SECRETS

ROMEO ALEXANDER

ROMEO ALEXANDER

Editing by Jo Bird
Beta reading by Melissa R

CID

The low hum of the mini-fridge near his feet was perfectly pleasant. Still, Cid was convinced the random ticking noise it made was going to drive him crazy. It wasn't helped by the rattle that came from the vent every time the heat came on or when it turned off for some reason.

While he wasn't confident he could do anything about the mini-fridge, Cid found his eyes sweeping up to the vent overhead. He looked around the lobby, even getting up to peer over the front desk.

Nope, Greenford University's Medical Clinic was completely and utterly empty of anyone except him, just as it had been for the past three hours. He had already swept and mopped the gray tiled floor, making it so clean he'd swear someone could eat off it. He'd vacuumed the rug leading from the front door to the desk and then the plush waiting room chairs. He'd even dusted the dangling ceiling fans and wiped down the pictures that showed the changes at the university over the past century.

But that damned rattle was going to drive him crazy.

Cid glanced over his shoulder toward the partially open

door to the right of the desk. It led to a hallway where the examination rooms waited, as well as the offices for the senior medical doctors on staff. He knew for a fact that the doctor on duty, Dr. Finn, was busy with something in her office and wouldn't check on him for a while.

Or he hoped anyway, as he pulled one of the waiting room chairs over and set it beneath the vent. It was built into the ducts that ran along the back of the room, and though he was pretty tall, he still needed the extra few inches to reach it. With that done, he dug out the small tool kit from the bottom drawer of the desk and, after searching for a moment, grabbed a screwdriver.

Cid removed the screws and carefully pulled the vent faceplate off before setting it aside as quietly as possible. He pulled his phone out of his pocket, turned on the flashlight and craned his neck to look around inside the vent.

"Ah-ha," he mumbled into the vent. "You're the little bastard causing the problem."

There was a small fan just a little way down the vent to help circulate the air. From what he could see in the light from his phone, the bolt holding it in place was loose.

Chuckling to himself, he rooted through the tool kit and grabbed what he needed. The only problem, he quickly found, was that to reach the bolt with the tool, he needed to practically shove himself into the vent. Standing on the tips of his toes, he pushed his arm through the opening and fought to catch the bolt with the tool. He came close, but nothing definitive other than a few clangs and bumps as he tried to maneuver his arm blindly.

"Why," came the familiar voice of Dr. Finn, "am I not surprised to find you committing a workplace violation while unsupervised?"

Cid froze. "Uh, hi, Dr. Finn...whatcha, whatcha doin'?"

"Watching you try to kill yourself in order to...what exactly are you doing?"

"Fixing the rattle in the vent that's been threatening to drive me crazy, like really crazy, for ages now?"

"You don't sound so sure."

"I'm sure. Like, pretty sure. I'm just not sure how much trouble I'm in for getting busted."

The woman chuckled. "Of course, because you got caught. Not because you were doing anything wrong, no, you're worried because you got in trouble."

Personally, he thought the trick to breaking the rules, at least the little ones, was not to get caught. Otherwise, was he *really* breaking the rules? Then again, he supposed that also hailed back to the age-old conundrum of whether or not a tree made a sound when it fell if no one was around to hear it. Of course, it did. Soundwaves still existed, whether or not there was anyone there to hear it.

So he supposed she could argue that whether or not he was caught, breaking the rules was breaking the rules. Then again, he could also argue that rules weren't the same as soundwaves. One followed the rules of physics, the other the rules of man. Yet, he had to admit that both had their own way of affecting reality, one through immutable forces and laws and the other through guiding behavior, which really made it subjective.

"Cid!" Dr. Finn called, sounding exasperated.

Cid blinked, realizing he was still shoulder deep in the vent and couldn't see her. "Uh, yeah?"

"Do I want to know what you were just thinking about?"

"Oh. Um, I guess I could sum it up as the subjective versus objective nature of reality?"

Dr. Finn sighed. "Get your arm out of the vent, and get

off the chair. And no, I do not need to know precisely how you got from being caught to suddenly philosophizing about the nature of reality."

Which was fair, as he would have been more than ready to explain it to her, just as he had several dozen times in the past. His mind had a tendency to wander down random tangents, which always started off at perfectly normal places. Problem was, he tended to make mental leaps along the way and would inevitably end up somewhere that, from an outside perspective, made absolutely no sense. It always required him to backtrack and have to explain how he'd gone from A to J.

He did as he was told, though, and pulled his arm free, albeit a little reluctantly as he hadn't managed to fix the loose bolt. Dr. Finn was standing by the doorway leading deeper into the clinic, and he was relieved to see an amused expression on her face despite the crossed arms.

"I thought you'd be busy for a little while," he explained, hopping off the chair.

"Which is your excuse for why you were in the vent instead of raising a maintenance ticket?"

"Aw," he whined. "You know they take forever to fix anything unless it's a dire emergency."

"Yes," she said patiently. "I'm sure they have more important things to do than to go running around fixing every rattling vent."

He was of the mind that it would take someone with the right tools and training all of thirty seconds to fix something like that but knew there was no point in arguing. Even if it would probably take a year for someone to show up, he had technically been doing something he wasn't supposed to do, and that was probably the topic to focus on.

"Sorry," he said, grabbing the faceplate and standing up to put it back into place. "It was driving me crazy."

"Are you really that bored?" Dr. Finn asked.

"Yeah."

She stepped around the chair as he tightened the last screw into place, looking around. "Well, this place is certainly gleaming. It's so clean. I'm fairly certain you did more cleaning in here than the cleaning staff is supposed to do in a week."

"I tried organizing the patient files, but the system kept telling me I needed admin access to even move stuff around," Cid complained, hopping down off the chair.

"The last time you 'organized' anything in here, we couldn't find alcohol swabs or thermometers for a whole weekend while you were away," Dr. Finn pointed out as Cid dragged the chair back to its rightful place against the wall.

Cid sighed heavily. "They were with the bandages and aspirin."

"Which you put at the bottom of the cabinet in the storage room. Where we put the excess stuff."

"Which I put in the extra storage, where it belongs! My way made sense."

"Your way completely threw us off."

Which was precisely why he wasn't allowed to organize anything anymore. Well, that wasn't strictly true, he was allowed so long as he was being supervised and any 'signifi- cant changes' he proposed had to be approved by the physi- cian in charge.

"This is discrimination," Cid complained.

Dr. Finn snorted. "Really? Based on what?"

"I don't know...like uh...I don't know."

She patted his shoulder consolingly. "When you're a big

boy doctor who doesn't need someone to watch over you to make sure you don't get into trouble, I'm sure you'll be able to organize all the things you want without being fussed at."

"I've heard horror stories," Cid told her. "I'm not pissing off nurses."

"Well, it's good that you've learned that sooner rather than later. Some doctors never learn it and they wonder why their work lives are absolute hell."

Cid sighed and flopped back into the seat behind the desk. Honestly, he wasn't all that frustrated with Dr. Finn or the rule against organizing stuff. He truly enjoyed his work at the clinic, and he counted himself lucky for landing such a great place for his residency. Dr. Finn and Dr. Wartburton were excellent physicians, and they were generally enjoyable people to work under and learn from. The clinic was a great place to learn, especially since Cid's plan was to become a family doctor, and a range of different student problems gave him the sort of practice he would need.

"You know," Dr. Finn said, sitting on the edge of the desk. "Both Rich and I have told you that you can bring in a tablet or use your phone for music when it's slow like this. If we don't need someone on alert, then you're perfectly allowed to sit back and relax."

"I forgot my bag at home," Cid muttered, adjusting the mouse pad so it sat perfectly perpendicular to the edge of the desk. "And I'm waiting for my replacement phone to come in."

Dr. Finn glanced at the phone on the desk. "Then what's that?"

"My phone. Doesn't work, though. Not like...as a phone."

"Oh right, that's the one you dropped into a...puddle?"

"Plastic pool that someone had in their backyard for the dogs."

"Right. And you were sober for that."

Cid sighed heavily. "Completely and utterly. Now it doesn't get a signal, can't type for crap on it, so there's no music or audiobooks for me until the new phone comes in. Flashlight works, though! So there's that."

"Which allowed it to work just enough to get you into trouble." She chuckled. "You're too restless for your own good sometimes."

It was said affectionately, but Cid cringed inwardly at the sheer truth of it. For as long as he could remember, he had been operating at a speed that wore other people down. At best, people were fondly exasperated, at worst, they were aggravated and tried to spend as little time around him as possible. Sometimes people found his behavior fascinating or endearing, but he'd grown pretty used to people finding it annoying as well.

"Trust me," Cid assured her, fiddling with the keyboard to straighten it. "I've heard that *a lot* growing up."

"Among some other more colorful, and probably less kind phrases as well," Dr. Finn said knowingly.

He laughed. "Yeah, something like that."

Yet he'd like to think he'd learn to deal with people's criticisms pretty well. When his parents died at a young age, Cid had been left without any family and, inevitably, was tossed into the system. And while some children had been lucky to find long-term homes or even been adopted, Cid had found himself staying in the foster care system until he'd turned eighteen.

It wasn't like his time in the system had been bad necessarily. Actually, he'd had a few good foster homes over the years that he remembered fondly. The rest were genuinely fine, taking care of his needs and making sure he was at least healthy and relatively happy. But the constant moving around between states, towns, and homes, had done little to soothe his own restless nature.

Sometimes he wondered if he'd ever learn to settle down, and other times if settling down was even what he was looking for.

"Oh!" Dr. Finn straightened suddenly, eyes brightening. "I forgot to ask how your date went this past weekend."

Cid shrugged. "Nothing worth talking about, ya know? He was nice. He said I was nice. We were nice."

"But nothing sparked, huh?"

Cid shrugged. "I guess that's the best way to put it. Pretty sure I talked him under the table and he was ready to run within the first fifteen minutes."

Dr. Finn laughed softly. "I think you're being hard on yourself."

"Or honest," he corrected.

"You're young, well-educated, and intelligent."

"Bit redundant, wouldn't you say?"

She laughed again. "No, there is a mile's worth of difference between being educated and being smart. You should know that by now."

"True," Cid said slowly, thinking of a few of the people he'd shared classes with over the years. "But go on, you were extolling my virtues and my poor little ego was loving it."

She kicked him gently. "I'm serious. You're a smart guy, and you're not exactly lacking in the looks department."

"Wow," Cid said, eyes going wide. "Nothing quite like my boss telling me I'm hot to get my day started."

"It's close to ending, actually," she corrected with a glance at her wristwatch. "And even your boss can see and know a good-looking man when she sees one. I'm not exactly blind."

Cid laughed at that, swatting her foot away when she gave him another jab with the toe of her shoe. He wasn't so modest as to deny what she was saying, but he wasn't going to outright admit it either. He didn't think he was *that* vain.

"You're not exactly bad looking yourself," he pointed out, giving her foot another swat when it came in for another jab.

"Ah," she sighed deeply. "If only I was a few years younger...and not your boss, we could make things work out so well."

"Well, and the fact that you're only into women and I'm only into men," he pointed out, watching her leg carefully.

She hummed thoughtfully. "You're right. It would never work out between us. Oh, and your hair is a mess."

Almost immediately, he turned to the nearby blank computer screen and checked his hair. There wasn't a hair out of place, which was an achievement considering he'd probably been absently running his hands through it for the longest time. That didn't stop him from looking over the pale blond locks, turning his head from side to side to make sure that it wasn't, in fact, messed up.

"My hair is fine," Cid complained, running a hand down his temple and over his stubbled jaw. He had considered keeping the stubble. He thought it went a long way toward accenting his narrow jaw and made it look more defined.

"Yes, but it's fun to watch you panic when you think you have a hair out of place," she laughed.

It was his turn to kick her, albeit gently. Okay, maybe he was *a little* vain. Enough to care if his appearance got marred, at least when he wasn't working. If he had to focus on a task, especially helping a patient, he didn't care one bit what got on him or messed with his appearance.

"The Pretty Doctor," Dr. Finn recited to him, grinning wide.

Cid groaned, waving her off. "Oh, don't start that."

"Isn't that what that girl called you? Pretty sure it was."

Cid sighed, knowing there was no chance in hell he was going to get her to go away now that she had smelled blood in the water. "Yes, and I really wish Derrick hadn't felt the need to tell you about that either. Like, I really wish he hadn't."

Dr. Finn chuckled. "Imagine how poor Derrick felt when he got to overhear one of his patients say she wished she'd gotten The Pretty Doctor. You know, the one with the baby blues?"

Cid sighed, feeling warm from both embarrassment and a little boost to his ego. It was awkward to be praised on his looks through indirect sources like that, especially since everyone thought it was the funniest thing. Yet he wasn't immune to the compliment all the same. He would have just been far happier if the compliment had been given in person...and by a good-looking guy.

"Tell you what," Dr. Finn said, leaning forward. "If you promise to go out and have yourself a good time tonight, I'll let you off early. *And* I'll even make sure you work a later shift tomorrow instead of your morning one."

Cid perked up at that. With medical school all but behind him, he could justify using his free time for enjoyable things instead of non-stop studying and worrying over grades and test scores. So if he was going to be offered a free Friday night, along with the time needed the next day to recover in case the night got a little crazy, he was definitely going to take the opportunity.

"I might be willing to agree to that," Cid said, barely managing to keep the eagerness out of his voice. "But that doesn't mean I'm going to try to look for a date or anything. Just...no."

She laughed. "Of course not. You're probably going to end up at some club or bar, getting drunk, and hopefully not making too big a fool of yourself. That's not the time or place for looking for dates."

That had definitely been his plan. "Well, I might be young, Dr. Finn, but I'm not stupid enough to think I'm going to find a long-term relationship in a club."

"Good," she said, hopping off the desk. "Then get your ass out of here before you find more trouble to get into. I expect to see you for the afternoon shift tomorrow, though."

Cid gave her a lazy salute as he stood up, grabbing his phone off the desk and making for the front door.

ALEX

Bending over, Alex peered into the mop bucket, sighing at the water that was already rapidly darkening. The warm weather had brought a great deal of rain and, inevitably, mud. It didn't matter how many times he mopped the floors, there was always another set of muddy footprints to clean up as the students roamed the halls of Greenford University.

He honestly didn't think it would be much longer until he had to replace the bucket of bleach water once more. His supervisor had tried telling him over the past few weeks that it wasn't necessary to do it every time the water got dark, the bleach would still clean, and the mop would still wipe up the mud. For Alex, though, he just couldn't wrap his head around the idea of a floor getting clean after being soaked in dirty water, bleach or no bleach.

It was Friday, so that meant he was scheduled to go through the science building and keep the place clean, even if it did feel like an uphill battle. It would grow a little easier near the end of his shift when the number of students dropped dramatically with only a few evening classes left.

He looked up as the relatively quiet hallway came to life with the sound of footsteps and chatter. A stream of students poured out of one of the doors further down, most barely glanced in his direction as they passed. A wave of amusement ran through him as he watched the eyes of a gaggle of female students linger on him as they walked.

When they were close, he glanced up, unable to help his curiosity. They were young, which he expected, probably in their early twenties. When it came to women, Alex wasn't terribly picky. They just had to be good-looking for him to be interested. Of the group, a couple of them certainly drew his eye, and he smirked when one of them laughed lightly, cheeks turning pink as their eyes met.

They were around the corner and out of sight a minute later. If it wasn't for the fact that he was supposed to be behaving himself, he would have been sorely tempted to stop them and have a little chat. But he wasn't supposed to draw attention to himself, and he imagined that sleeping his way through the willing members of the student body probably fell under that.

When he felt a strong vibration coming from his pocket, Alex gave another heavy sigh. He knew how his luck worked and he had a fairly good idea who was calling him. When he pulled out his phone, sure enough, he saw the familiar name across the screen.

Rolling his eyes, he glanced around to make sure the coast was clear before answering it. "Ken."

"Agent Drayfus," Ken corrected, though he sounded more resigned than irritated. "Just doing my weekly checkup."

"Well, Ken," Alex said with a grin. "Seeing as how I'm talking to you and not screaming in pain, I'm going to guess I'm doing alright."

"Very cute."

"Although, if it was possible to die from boredom, I'd be on my way."

Ken chose to ignore him. "Anything worth reporting?"

"Some good-looking people on this campus," Alex said, leaning against the wall behind him and keeping an eye out for a professor or his supervisor. "But I'm guessing that's not what you're asking."

"It would do you well to take this a little more seriously," Ken warned him. "If you can't bring yourself to follow the rules and guidelines we gave you, we can always pull you back into direct supervision again."

Alex groaned. "Jesus, not that shit again. Six months of it and I felt like I was going to lose my fucking mind."

"Then take this a little more seriously. These check-ins are important, and you need to start treating them that way," Ken told him.

Alex sighed, knowing the federal agent was right but still hating it all the same. He'd spent most of his life being fairly independent. Even as a child, his absent father and useless mother had meant he was pretty much operating on his own. There had been only his younger brother, Rio, that Alex had ever been beholden to, devoted really.

Well, and the Los Muertos.

"Seen any of your old friends?" Ken asked as if sensing his thoughts.

Alex's grip on his phone tightened. "No, and they're not my friends."

Ken hummed thoughtfully. "We haven't seen any outward activity from them either. If they're looking for you, they're keeping to the city limits."

Which was good because Alex was a few hour's drive from Port Dale, where Los Muertos had claimed several neighborhoods as their territory. His old apartment, the one he'd shared with his younger brother and their drug-addled mother, had been in one of those territories. There weren't many options for someone like Alex growing up, and doing some running and dealing for them was the best way to keep safe, and by proxy, help to shield his brother as well.

Of course, all that safety had gone right out the window when Alex had turned coat and decided to play star witness for the trial of the head of the Los Muertos gang, Luis. Alex might not have been an official member of the Los Muertos gang, but they had certainly used him as much as possible, knowing he would do quite a lot to keep the umbrella of protection around his family. In the years he'd helped the gang, doing things he hated and would never take pride in, he'd seen quite a lot and so had plenty of information that would cause a lot of trouble if he went to court.

Which was precisely why the Los Muertos wanted his head on a platter. Personally, Alex didn't care about that too much, not so long as he got to do a lot of damage to the Los Muertos before he went down. They might regard him as a traitor and a snitch, but they hadn't kept their promises either, so he considered it a fair trade.

They'd killed his brother, and he was going to make sure they hurt.

"I'm taking it seriously," Alex finally told the agent, taking a deep breath. "And I don't want to go back to hiding in some random house in the middle of nowhere, with nothing but your agents for company. Seriously."

"Then you know what you have to do," Ken told him simply.

Alex nodded. "There's nothing worth reporting. No one's followed me, asked any weird questions, nothing like that. Hell, I'm a janitor at some university. No one here gives a shit about me."

Well, other than to give him a quick look over anyway. But that was something he wasn't unfamiliar with either. Alex was completely honest about what he looked like and wasn't afraid to use it to his advantage, or rather to whatever advantage he needed.

"Just don't draw attention to yourself," Ken warned once more. "By yourself, you draw enough as it is. Don't let your personality or your dick get in the way."

Alex had to chuckle at that. "I've been behaving, and I've been keeping a low profile, alright?"

And he really had, much to his continuing frustration. The weather was warming up, but he always wore a long sleeve shirt whenever he was out in public. That did wonders to cover up the myriad of tattoos that coated both of his arms, shoulders, and back. It didn't hide the thick muscles that corded his arms or the ones peeking up around his neck, but it hid the worst of them.

Alex had also been careful to keep his behavior under control as well. Because Ken was right, Alex *did* naturally draw attention, if only because of the sheer size of him. It was one reason the Los Muertos had enjoyed sending Alex along with gang members for *negotiations*. Alex towered over most people, and between keeping himself active and a genetic boost from his father, he was built like a tank. Add in the square jaw, dark eyes, and his tendency to keep his hair military-style short, and he was an imposing and atten-tion-grabbing presence.

"I've been here for six months, and I've only gotten laid once," Alex assured him.

"You should probably avoid it all together," Ken said, but he didn't sound too insistent.

"I know," Alex promised, trying to sound genuine.

The warning trickled out of his head when the same door from before opened and a young man stepped out into the hall. He was on the short side, with messy chestnut hair that hung over his eyes as he stared down at his phone as he walked. The young man looked up when he caught sight of Alex, eyes widening and a small smile quirking his lips.

Alex watched him go, eyes drifting down to the curve of the man's ass that was perfectly cupped by his jeans. The young man wasn't really Alex's type, generally preferring guys built a little less fragile, but Alex wouldn't have sent him away from his bed either.

"Alex?" Ken's voice came through the phone, sounding annoyed. "What are you doing?"

"Standing in a hallway at work, hoping I don't get caught on my phone," Alex lied, watching the young man disappear around the corner. "Going to be hard to tell my supervisor that I'm talking to a federal agent."

"Say it a little louder," Ken growled. "Let everyone know. While you're at it, wear a shirt that says In Witness Protection. I'm sure that would go over quite well."

"I don't know," Alex said, glancing down the hall to make sure he was alone. "Some of these kids are into some very interesting shirts and slogans. They might not think twice about it."

"Kids," Ken repeated. "You're barely older than they are."

"I'm twenty-nine," Alex said. "That's old enough to call them kids."

"Almost thirty and you're busy trying to sleep around like one of those kids. Maybe you should try for something a little more meaningful," Ken suggested dryly.

"What? I'm supposed to keep it in my pants, but I'm allowed to go on dates?" Alex snorted.

"We can't stop you from doing either of those things. We just highly suggest you don't. A relationship with your circumstances would be...difficult," Ken admitted.

"Great. Well, I still have a shift to finish up and a night to plan."

"To plan? What did we just talk about?"

"Look, I can't just stay in that tiny ass apartment the whole time. If I wanted to do that, I would have stayed in that nice house you had me in with all your buddies watching me. Plus, there's supposed to be a killer strip club in town, and I want to see some asses shaking."

Ken sighed. "I really don't need the details."

"What? You don't want me to send you pictures?"

"No."

"You're no fun."

"But I'm good at what I do. Just keep a low profile."

Alex smirked. "I'll do my absolute best, promise."

"Good. Then we'll talk next week."

"Looking forward to it."

"I'm sure."

The line clicked off, and Alex tucked his phone away with a chuckle. The agent was too serious for his own good, but Alex couldn't blame him. In truth, he knew he should be taking things a little more seriously as well, or at least acting like he was. A whole group of murderous gang members wanted his head and had plenty of money to spare in finding him.

Still, it was either sit around and brood about his life all night when he wasn't working or risk putting himself out there. His life was a mess, utterly torn apart, and he had nothing left but himself and whatever time he had ahead of him. Really, so long as he lived long enough to hurt the Los Muertos, Alex would be okay with that.

And he wanted to see a nice rack or ass shaking itself across a dance floor.

"OH," Alex said in surprise, entering the main room of the strip club and staring at the stage.

It was a lot fancier than he was expecting. The central area, which looked like it served as a dance floor, also contained the stage near the back. The floor was some sort of glass, lit from beneath by multicolored lights.

The whole place was well lit and colorful, from the bars, one on each side of the room, to the banisters leading up to the second floor. Even the small tables situated near the back had lights on them, albeit with brightly colored shades in all colors of the rainbow.

But that wasn't what had surprised him. Instead, his eyes were locked on the man currently working himself quite expertly out of his pants on the stage. The guy was the very definition of twink, up to and including the wicked smile on his face as he bared his underwear-covered ass to the excited crowd.

"Something wrong?" a voice called from the bar.

Alex turned to the woman working the bar and shrugged. "When I heard this was a strip club..."

She laughed. "It is. We cater to all tastes around here. You missed one of our girls by a few minutes, now Danny Boy has got the stage."

"You guys do male and female strippers?" Alex asked in surprise.

"That we do. That a problem?" she asked, raising a brow.

Alex snorted. "The only problem I've got right now is the lack of alcohol in my system."

She grinned wickedly. "Tell you what, since it's your first time, I'll give you the virgin special."

"It better fuck better than a virgin," Alex called.

"You bet ya," she winked and disappeared behind the bar.

Alex turned his attention back to the stage as the stripper was now clad only in a pair of the tightest trunks Alex thought he'd ever seen. He'd honestly never heard of a co-ed strip club, but they weren't going to hear any complaints out of him.

"Here ya go," the bartender told him, handing over a tall glass of brightly colored drink. "On the house. Just this one time."

He laughed, raising the glass to her in a salute. "Cheers to you then."

Alex took a drink, finding it just a little sweet and sour, with a hint of something earthy under it all. He cleared his throat when it hit his stomach with what felt like a fireball, shaking his head.

"Damn, alright," he muttered.

Drink in hand, he turned his attention back to the stage, grinning widely as he watched the stripper. Honestly, one of the few good things about being under witness protection and away from the Los Muertos was that he got to indulge his tastes completely. The Los Muertos weren't exactly known for being compassionate and open-minded, and they would have been incredibly pissed to find out one of their own was fucking men as well as women.

Personally, Alex thought the attitude was stupid. Not

because of any 'acceptance', 'inclusion', or any other number of random buzzwords he'd heard thrown around on the campus. He just saw no point in getting hung up on where someone stuck their dick, at least so long as everyone involved was into it. If it felt good and wasn't hurting anyone, Alex didn't see an issue and enjoyed himself.

The gang mentality circled around it making guys *less of a man.* Alex could only snort at that. Most of those assholes couldn't have stood up to him in a fight and were fond of using Alex's sheer size and mean expression because their own sucked ass. Plus, he knew most of those assholes would cry if someone so much as stuck a finger up their ass, let alone Alex's dick. And he'd known quite a few guys out there who took him like a champ, so Alex wasn't too impressed by the whole toughness argument.

He was jerked out of his thoughts as a woman slammed into him. Grunting, he pulled his drink to his side to steady it against his body and hopefully prevent it from sloshing down his front. The woman, who was leaning heavily into him and flailing about, absolutely reeked of beer.

"Sorry," she slurred loudly. "I didn't see...you. Oh. Hi."

The last was said with a lazy grin as she peered up into his face. Alex bit back a groan as her hands came to rest on his chest and stomach, squeezing as she felt him up.

"Hi," he said, wondering if he could get away with nudging her off him without knocking her over in the process.

"You're cute," she informed him, the hand on his stomach threatening to move further south.

"Thanks," he told her, using his free hand to subtly stop her hand from moving down.

"Wanna go somewhere?" she asked, as blunt as she was wasted.

"You're uh, not really my type," he told her.

"Aw," she leaned back. "I always find the gay ones."

That wasn't quite what he meant. It had more to do with the fact that there was no way in hell he was sleeping with anyone as wasted as she was. The thought felt dirty in the worst way, and he was sure it wouldn't exactly be thrilling for either of them. And if she wanted to believe it was because he was gay, well, he would roll with that.

He glanced over at the bar. "Why don't we get you a ride home? I'm sure the bartender would help you."

The woman sighed heavily, one of her hands falling onto the top of his glass and almost spilling its contents as she leaned closer. "Sure you don't wanna give me a try anyway? It'll be fun."

Inwardly groaning, he slowly stepped toward the bar, hoping the grabby woman would follow him. Sure enough, she kept close, talking low enough that Alex couldn't understand her.

"What's up?" the bartender asked, eyeing the woman behind Alex.

"She's," Alex began but was interrupted as the woman's next step became a stumble and she had no choice but to grab the bar to keep herself upright. "Yeah. That."

"Friend of yours?"

Alex shook his head. "But I thought maybe you guys could call her a ride? Maybe?"

His eyes said please as he stared at her, but the bartender nodded, leaning over the bar to talk to the woman. Sensing his opportunity, he backed away before the drunk woman could notice. Shaking his head, he took a deep drink, trying to make his way through the crowd where he wouldn't be noticed.

After another couple of songs, he found himself in a

dark corner where he hoped he wouldn't be disturbed. He'd worked his way through about half his drink and was content to watch as the next stripper came on. This one was big, tall, and built strong, and Alex had to admit he was intrigued. The man's dance style was interesting, far less enticing than the last man's, and far more dominating.

Alex pushed away from the wall in the hopes of getting closer and stopped short as the room began to tilt. He shook his head, trying to clear his vision. If anything, that only served to make the room spin harder, twisting his stomach as he reached out to balance himself on a nearby table.

"Jesus," he muttered, looking down at his glass. "How much alcohol did she put in this thing?"

Apparently enough to make him feel like he'd downed half a fifth, or maybe even more. He considered himself more than capable of holding his alcohol, but it felt like he'd been drinking on an empty stomach.

"Not good," he muttered, setting his glass on the nearby table and stumbling his way toward the door.

His thought was that a dose of fresh air would do him good. It was still Spring, which meant the nighttime air would be cool and might slap some sense into him. If that didn't work, he could always try to find a ride home.

He managed to shuffle his way outside, though he was forced to lean against the side of the building as he made his way down the sidewalk. His only thoughts were that the drink packed too much of a punch and that maybe if he got to his car, he might be able to rest and get his head on straight.

Remembering where the car was parked was a different matter altogether. Rather than purposefully, if slowly, making his way to where he'd parked his car, Alex found himself stumbling blindly down the sidewalk, head spinning too hard for him to think clearly.

"Fuck," he muttered, clutching the nearest wall to keep himself upright.

He was losing consciousness, and fast.

CID

Among the pounding beat of the music vibrating his skin, he felt an elbow push into his side. Cid glanced over at his friend Alice, who was grinning widely at him. He knew that smile all too well and was sure the next words out of her mouth were probably going to be scandalous.

Alice nodded across the club. "Would you suck his dick?"

Yeah, that was about right.

Cid dutifully looked across the room, trying to peer through the sea of people to understand what man she was talking about. There were plenty of good-looking guys in the club, but he knew his friend. Alice wouldn't choose someone for that question unless they were drop-dead gorgeous or there was something else that stood out about them.

Then he caught sight of who he thought it was. "The guy with a man bun and a tie-dye shirt?"

Alice smirked. "That's the one."

"Not my type," Cid informed her, leaning back against the bench and taking a sip from his drink.

Alice rolled her eyes. "You're telling me you only suck the dicks of guys who are perfectly your type?"

"No," Cid admitted. "But there's still plenty of other guys here I would choose first. I hate man-buns."

"You hate long hair on guys."

He wouldn't necessarily say hate, but he wasn't a fan of long hair on men, that was true. Truthfully, he liked short hair on guys, especially if it was the sort that felt bristly or stubbly against his fingertips as he ran his hands over their head.

Alice finally rolled her eyes. "If you're not going to pick anyone up, then we might as well head out."

"And go where?" Cid asked, not taking the bait about hooking up.

Her devious grin didn't abate in the slightest. "I know you haven't been to Nocturne before."

Cid groaned. "C'mon, Alice. I told you, like, a dozen times, I'm not really into strippers."

"How would you know if you've never seen them?"

"I've seen them!"

"Drunk twinks at a gay club trying to shake their asses doesn't count."

There was really only one way to get out of this conversation without hearing it come up again, and that was to go along with her idea. Alice was a lovely woman, full of joy and a lot of passion for life, but that didn't change the fact that she was as hardheaded as they came. Once she had an idea in her head, Cid suspected not even God himself could make her change her mind.

Alice leaned closer, wagging her brow. "And I hear one of the dancers on tonight is this big guy. Tall, dark, handsome as hell, and apparently dances like he's going to fuck you into walking funny."

Cid would have been lying if he'd tried to claim that the description didn't sound appealing to him. One of the greatest frustrations in his dating and sex life had been that everyone looked at him and automatically assumed that he was the one doing the topping. His only hope was to find someone about his size or taller, hard enough on its own since he was well above average height, and hope that they too weren't a bottom.

"Well," Cid relented, draining his drink. "I guess I should see it once, right?"

Alice practically cackled, clapping her hands together with glee. "Awesome. I'm so buying you a private dance."

Cid laughed, swatting at her as he edged out from the booth. "Don't you dare! I don't need some sweaty guy's crotch shoved in my face."

"As opposed," Alice began, hopping up onto Cid's back, "to the other guys who have shoved their sweaty crotches into your face."

Cid waited until she had a good grip on him before continuing forward. "Yeah, but they weren't paid for by my shithead of a friend."

"Details, details," she told him as he made his way through the crowd and out the double doors.

Honestly, he didn't have anything against strippers, he just didn't see the appeal. Even if they were good at what they did, what did that matter? One of his foster fathers, in a bout of drunkenness, had once said that going to see a strip show was just a way to get fucked without having sex, and Cid couldn't argue with the logic. If he was going to get to see a good-looking guy with little clothing, he'd prefer it be in the privacy of someone's bedroom with the promise of more to come.

"You planning on staying up there?" Cid asked, glancing over his shoulder.

"People move for you," Alice pointed out. "When they're not too busy gawking at you anyway. My short ass isn't going to get anyone to move. I gotta slip between them like a pickpocket."

"You're pocket-size," Cid told her, holding onto her legs as he walked down the sidewalk.

"My ex-boyfriend liked to call me a sit n' spin."

"Do I want to know why?"

"I'm sure if you use your imagination, you can probably figure out why."

Cid shook his head. "It's nice to know you have a classy taste in men."

"I sure do know how to pick 'em," Alice said confidently.

Cid chuckled as they turned the corner onto the next block, growing closer to Nocturne. He honestly didn't know if he was going to end up enjoying himself all that much, but at least he could count on drinks and good company.

Alice chuckled in his ear. "Damn, and I thought *I* was drinking pretty heavy tonight."

Cid peered over his shoulder once more, frowning. "What are you talking about? I'm barely buzzed."

Alice snorted, pointing across the street. "Not you, him."

Cid followed her arm until he saw the man. The guy was barely keeping to his feet and as he watched, the stranger sank down to his knees, back hunched with the tell-tale signs of heaving.

"Jesus," Cid said, slowing down to watch the man.

"God, is he about to pass out? Hope he pukes first," Alice said, still snickering.

"Alice, that's not a good thing," Cid chided, checking both sides of the street.

"People drink too much. It happens," Alice told him.

Cid made up his mind as the man wobbled on all fours, looking ready to fall over at a moment's notice. He stepped off the sidewalk after making sure no cars were coming.

"And people die from drinking too much all the time too," Cid told her.

"You're off to play doctor, aren't you?" she asked wryly.

"I *am* a doctor," Cid reminded her.

Alice sighed but didn't argue as Cid mounted the sidewalk and approached the man. Without thinking, Cid shook her off his back before kneeling down. The timing was impeccable as the man's heaving finally resulted in a wet sound as he spilled the contents of his stomach onto the sidewalk.

"Oh, God," Alice groaned, stepping away. "I can't. Fuck me."

Cid inched closer, hoping to get the man's attention once the first few heaves were done. "Sir?"

The man looked at him, eyes dazed, jaw clenched. "Who the fuck are you?"

"I'm a doctor. And it looks like you have a bad case of alcohol poisoning," Cid told him.

The man gave a shaky laugh. "Can't. Only had one. Not even one."

"My ass," Alice muttered from several feet away.

Cid got closer, slowly reaching out to press his fingers to the man's neck gently. The guy tensed but didn't do much more as Cid counted the pulses, watching his glowing wristwatch as he waited. He frowned, placing his hand over the man's chest and feeling his chest rise and fall.

"Why don't you sit back for me, sir?" Cid asked.

The man did as he was told, flopping against the wall with a snort. "Only people who call me sir are the ones I'm sticking my dick in. "

"Duly noted," Cid told him, the corner of his mouth twitching.

The man squinted at him, head weaving vaguely from side to side. "But if you're down, I am, you're kinda cute...really cute."

Cid ignored Alice's quiet laughter. "Well, you're aware enough to know that, I suppose."

The stranger's eyes closed almost completely as he stared up at Cid. "My name's...uh..."

Cid waited for a moment. "Do you know your name?"

That brought a round of watery chuckles from the other man. "Fuckin'...I don't know anymore."

Cid's brow furrowed, and he checked the man's pulse one more time. "Give yourself a minute."

"Alex," the man finally said, drawing out the end in a low slur.

"Well, hi, Alex, I'm Cid. And are you sure you only had one?"

That earned a derisive snort. "Didn't even finish the one I started...started with."

Cid waited as the man trailed off, eyelids growing heavy. "Did you leave your drink alone at any time?"

"No, fucker was in my hand the whole time."

"So you had your eyes on it all the time?"

The question brought on another dazed look, which Cid knew was due to a drunken thought. Eventually, the man shook his head. "I don't know. Maybe? Probably?"

"Well, if you only had one, and you're like this. It's probably a good idea that we get you to the hospital," Cid informed him, watching his eyes carefully.

"Drink was...too strong," Alex muttered, eyes again fluttering closed.

Cid spoke loudly, getting his attention and trying to hold it. "Well, don't let that one drink get you down. Think you can focus on my face?"

Alex's eyes opened again, peering steadily up at Cid. "It is a good face."

Cid laughed softly. "Glad you think so. Alice?"

"Yeah?" his friend asked, bending closer when he motioned for her.

"Call an ambulance. I think he's been drugged," Cid muttered to her. "Probably GHB, but tell them I can't be completely sure."

Alice pulled away and Cid turned his attention back to the man. "Sir?"

"Alex."

"Alex," Cid corrected himself. "I've got a really strong feeling you were given something other than just alcohol tonight."

"Fuck," Alex grunted succinctly, dark eyes opening to glower up at Cid. "Someone date raped me? The fuck?"

"The fuck indeed," Cid confirmed.

He couldn't be entirely sure, but he was confident. If the man was telling the truth, then something else had to come into play.

"You didn't have anything other than part of your drink tonight?" Cid asked, hearing Alice talking softly on the phone behind him.

Alex tried to shake his head but managed only to limply loll it from one side to the other. "Say no to drugs...okay, pot's okay...maybe a little bit of coke."

Cid chuckled softly. "And did you do any of those?"

"Naw. Been real good lately, gotta be a good boy. Or else Ken is gonna kick my ass."

"Ken your...friend? Brother?"

Alex's eyes opened again with a heated flash. "*Not* my brother."

It was the most energy he'd seen out of him, but Cid didn't think he wanted to provoke the man further. Anger might be good at keeping someone conscious and relatively alert, but someone who was essentially wasted was also not someone you wanted too pissed off either.

"He's my...babysitter," Alex muttered finally, head slumping down again.

"Parole officer?" Cid asked without a trace of judgment in his voice.

Alex peered up at him again, the corner of his mouth twitching. "What's up, Doc? You see me and think I'm trouble?"

"No," Cid said, shaking his head. "Just making conversation."

"Suuure," Alex drew out with a slur heavy enough to distort the word.

Looking at the other man now, Cid could understand Alex's doubt. Even slumped against the wall, Alex was bigger than Cid. He couldn't exactly be sure just how much bigger, at least in terms of height, but he guessed the man had about forty, maybe fifty pounds on him, and all muscle. His features, though slack from the alcohol and drugs in his system, were strong and fierce, and his face seemed prone to slipping into scowls.

"Not my job to judge you on your life," Cid told him. "Just to make sure you get to the hospital in one piece."

Alex groaned. "One of those fancy doctors then."

That gave Cid a chuckle. He couldn't quite picture himself as being fancy.

"I think that's the ambulance," Alice informed him softly.

Sure enough, the large vehicle pulled up to the curb next to them, and two men hopped out. Cid quickly backed up, telling them what he'd found out so far, though knowing they would do all their own checks on the way. He fidgeted next to Alice as they loaded the man onto a gurney and into the back of the ambulance.

"Fuck," Alex groaned loudly. "Fuckin' bright in here, what the hell? Don't you have a dimmer switch?"

"Sheesh," Alice muttered next to him. "I would've thought he would be passed out by now."

Cid smiled at that. "I was watching him fight the whole time. He seems pretty stubborn."

Alice eyed him. "You know you can't go with them, right?"

Cid glanced at her in surprise. "What? Yeah, I know that. Yeah, of course."

Alice rolled her eyes. "You look like you're ready to hop in the back and keep trying to help him."

"I do not."

"Yes, you do."

Cid let out a disgruntled huff. "Alright, maybe I do a little. I feel bad."

"And now he's off to the hospital to get either his stomach pumped or treated for whatever someone gave him," Alice said, frowning. "Or whatever he took himself."

"You think he did it to himself?" Cid asked curiously.

Alice shrugged. "Might be. I don't want to look at someone and automatically think 'criminal' but..."

"You're going to anyway," Cid finished with a snort.

She sighed. "And maybe you're right, and he's some poor bastard who someone decided to dose with something. Though I don't know why."

It was Cid's turn to shrug. "Simple. Guy that size? You'd want him drugged up and helpless if you were going to do something to him."

"So you think someone did drug him?"

"Like I told him, I'm not here to judge."

And honestly, he hoped the man had been honest when he'd talked about how little he'd drunk and having apparently taken no drugs. Lying patients were one of the greatest banes of emergency care. If the doctors or nurses didn't know what the person had in their system, they ran the risk of making the problem worse.

"Well," Alice said, looping her arm through his. "You've done your good deed for the day. So let's go see some strippers shake what their mama's gave them."

"Seriously?" Cid asked as he was dragged forward. "I'm almost completely sure that's where he just came from."

"Yeah, and?"

"The place where he might have been drugged."

Alice laughed, continuing to pull him along. "Then just don't order any drinks, simple."

ALEX

Squatting down, Alex let out a soft groan as a lance of pain shot through his head. He managed to catch himself on a nearby shelf in the storage room he was in. There were plenty of them scattered about Greenford's campus, and he'd gone digging around for a spare spray bottle to use since the last one had broken on him.

The nurses at the hospital had warned him he might suffer from a few side effects after they'd released him early Saturday morning. Which had included the headache that refused to go away. They'd also warned him he should probably take a day or two off work, but that part of the advice he had ignored.

"I swear to God," he muttered, rubbing his forehead.

He honestly could not believe he'd been drugged, *him*. Who the hell would want to drug him? It wasn't like someone was going to have much luck in dragging him into a car and into their house to have their way with him. Anyone big enough to do that would probably have a fair chance of forcing him directly. Then again, he'd also seen his fair share of messed up people in his life and knew that some people just got off on date rape.

Alex was glad he'd been capable of getting himself out of the club and onto the street. It might not have been a safer place overall, but it might have spared him from being noticed by whoever had laced his drink. He was pretty sure the bartender was safe. Otherwise, the place wouldn't still be in business. Thing was, he didn't have a long list of suspects either since he hadn't seen anyone near his drink.

"Doing alright in there?"

The familiar voice of his supervisor brought Alex up straight, earning him another dose of pain down the center of his skull. Grunting, he turned to find the older man standing in the hallway just outside the storage room. Archy was pushing sixty but built like a bodybuilder who was currently enjoying his twenties. Alex wanted to like the man. He was no-nonsense, hardworking, and cared about quality work.

There was just one problem.

"Just trying to find an empty spray bottle," Alex told him.

Archy's hard eyes swept over him, thin brow arching. "Hope so. Last person I found groaning in one of these closets, they were shooting up."

"I don't do that shit, boss," Alex told him.

"Better hope not. I brought you on because you looked like you need the work, but right now, it looks like you had yourself a little too much fun last night."

Right along with being no-nonsense, Archy also happened to be stubborn and a little on the judgmental side. He had taken one look at Alex and apparently determined he was trouble waiting to happen. Why the man had decided to take him on as a member of the sanitation crew,

Alex couldn't quite figure out, especially if the guy thought he was a partying drug user.

Alex rubbed the back of his neck. "Would you believe I only had one drink?"

"You look like shit, so, no."

"It really was only one."

"Uh-huh."

Alex sighed, deciding to bite the bullet and admit the truth. "That someone dosed when I wasn't looking."

Archy's brow rose again. "You said you weren't doing drugs. Which is it?"

Alex groaned. "Archy...someone put it in there. No one with any brains is going to take GHB and drink at the same time. I sure as shit didn't put that in there."

He didn't need to take harder drugs to know which ones you definitely didn't mix with alcohol and GHB was right up there on the top three list as far as he knew. Whoever had dosed his drink had been a little heavy-handed it seemed, as the drug had started kicking in before he could finish his drink. The nurses had been more than happy to tell him that he could have easily ended up comatose if he had finished it. As it was, he felt like shit, his head felt like someone was wildly swinging a pickaxe around in his skull, and his memory after stumbling out of the club was blurry and a little hit or miss.

"Who the hell would drug you?"

"Someone with a sick sense of humor? I don't know. Maybe they just wanted me drugged. Feels like I slammed a liquor store last night."

Archy scowled at him. "Then what the fuck are you doing in here today?"

"What? Working," Alex protested.

"You supposed to be working after someone slips you

something?" Archy asked, crossing his thick arms over his chest.

Alex huffed. "No."

"Alright then. Get your ass home, but stop by the clinic on your way out. Make sure you aren't about to keel over like you look like you're about to."

"I'm fine Archy, I just have a headache."

"I wasn't asking," Archy told him, jabbing a finger at him. "About both things. Now get your ass out of here. I'll finish up your shift."

There was no way in hell he was going to try to argue with the older man. Shoulders slumping, he nodded and stepped out into the hallway when Archy stepped out of the way. The last thing he wanted to do was go back to his apartment and lay around feeling miserable. Not that going out anywhere was going to make him feel any better either. Going to work was his way of taking his mind off his misery.

Stepping out into the sunlight, he winced against the sudden blast of bright light. There were a few students lingering about just outside, where a few tables sat under the shade of a tall tree. It still faintly amused Alex to compare it to Port Dale, which had been big, metropolitan, and bordered by the sea, whereas Greenford...well, lived up to its name. The entire place seemed covered with greenery, from the old forests that lined it to the campus that tried to incorporate as many grassy clearings as possible and trees for people to enjoy when they went outside.

He had to dig his phone out of his pocket to pull up the app the campus had created a few years before. Alex wasn't familiar with the entire campus layout, and he'd never had to go to the clinic before. The app, at least, wasn't completely useless. After it had located him, he tapped the clinic in the list of options for a destination route and it mapped out his path for him. He looked it over for a moment, memorizing where he needed to go and locked his phone.

He stopped when his lock screen flashed onto the phone before going dark. It had only been a couple of years ago when Rio had insisted they go to the boardwalk in Port Dale. Alex had never been one for tourist traps, but his little brother had always been lighthearted and a little goofy, and he wanted to spend a day just screwing around with Alex at his side.

The picture had been taken by a stranger just as the sun was setting, leaving traces of orange and red on the horizon behind them. The Ferris wheel stationed at the center of the boardwalk was lit up brightly in the background. At the forefront were Alex and Rio, with Alex's arm slung over his brother's shoulders, the two of them grinning like fools as Rio held out a brightly colored drink named after a unicorn.

Alex's chest tightened at the memory and he hastily shoved his phone away before he was tempted to drag the picture, and others like it, out to stare at. He didn't want to get lost in nostalgia, regret, and sorrow, not while he was standing in the middle of the campus.

His brother, one of the only good things in Alex's life, was gone and there was no bringing him back. The best he could offer his brother was the chance to have some sort of revenge and bring justice down on the Los Muertos.

Yet if he was going to do that, he would have to make sure he was capable of standing on his own two feet. Archy's words echoed in his head, and with a deep, steadying breath, Alex shoved his memories aside and made for the clinic.

THE CLINIC WAS LOCATED at the front of the physical education building. A glance at the sign over the front of the building read Tom Eldon Building, but Alex was sure no one called it that. He'd never been to college in his life, but he doubted any student, adult or not, was going to call the buildings by their honorific names.

Entering the dimly lit lobby, he glanced around, finding a few doors, though all of them locked. To the right of the lobby was a wall of glass lit brightly from within. Over the door to the room was a brightly lit sign that read Greenford University Clinic and below it, Walk-ins and Appointments Welcome.

He hadn't even considered if he would need an appointment, so the sign was small comfort to him. Alex walked through the door into a clean and well-lit room, equipped with seating and a few portraits that looked like old pictures of the university.

"Hello?" Alex called, seeing that the front desk was empty.

There was a low thump followed by a yelp from the other side of the desk. A blond man jerked into view, rubbing the top of his head.

"Sorry, sorry," the man proclaimed, wincing. "Didn't hear you come in."

Alex forgot what he was going to say as he peered at the man. He was dressed in a doctor's coat thrown over a blue checkered button-up shirt. There was no denying the man was pretty young and very easy on the eyes. Even shadowed from his wincing, the man's eyes were a bright blue, and the faint blond stubble on his chin put his features somewhere between boy next door and trying to be a slightly grizzled professional.

"Wait," Alex said as the man's face eased. "I know you."

The guy looked up at him, eyes widening. "Oh! Hey, Alex, right?"

"Cid, right?"

"That's right, good memory."

"Huh," Alex said, looking the man over. "So, you are a doctor."

The other man grinned. "I am. Nice to see you on your feet. Guess you weren't in too bad shape, huh?"

Alex shrugged. "I don't even remember what they did. Pretty good memory of hurling a few times into a wastebasket, though."

"Yeah, you did that on the street," Cid chuckled. "But that's to be expected considering your condition."

Alex grimaced at that. "You'll be happy to know I wasn't just shitfaced and you were right, someone dosed me."

Cid wrinkled his nose. "Don't know why I'd be happy about that. You making an honest mistake and drinking too much is one thing, mistakes happen. But someone slipping something extra in your drink? That just worries me more."

"Yeah," Alex agreed, cocking his head.

Cid beamed, finally pulling his hand away from the back of his head. "But that's okay, I guess, since you're better, so that's good."

"Anyone ever told you that you repeat yourself?" Alex asked.

Cid chuckled, nodding his head vigorously. "Yeah, I do it when I'm...I don't know, wound up I guess is the word for it. I also forget what I'm saying and stumble over my words. My brain works faster than my mouth and I get tripped up a lot."

And apparently, he spoke at the speed of light from how quickly the man managed to spit out the explanation. It reminded him a bit of his brother actually, who had always been quick with a smile and spoke rapidly too. It had always been a good counterbalance to Alex's more serious, if sarcastic, attitude.

"Did I..." Alex began, inwardly wincing as he knew it was probably a good idea to get this out of the way, "say anything...weird or whatever, when you found me?"

Cid screwed his face up into a thoughtful expression, and Alex wondered if every emotion the man felt was so boldly broadcast. "No, not really. You were pretty out of it, though, so you were having a hard time stringing sentences together. Told me your name, that you hadn't taken anything more than a little bit of alcohol, oh and apparently your 'babysitter', Ken, was going to have some words with you."

"That's it?" Alex asked.

"Yeah, that's about it, yeah. Like I said, you were pretty out of it."

Alex nodded, relieved. "That's good. I tend to say...well, things, when I've had a bit to drink, and I thought being drugged might have the same effect."

Cid laughed at that, his blue eyes brightening with amusement. "Well, you did throw a couple things out there, but I wouldn't call them bad."

"What did I say?" Alex asked slowly, not sure if he wanted to know.

Cid winked. "You made a pass or two, nothing serious."

"Oh," Alex said with a sigh of relief. "Okay. Well, I probably came on a little strong, but there are worse things."

"Are there?" Cid asked, cocking his head. "Like what?"

Definitely not things like Cid had apparently heard. Even stone-cold sober, in a more casual setting, Alex would have been hard-pressed not to come onto the other man. Of course, he would have at least waited until he was sure he wasn't about to get himself into trouble by hitting on him first, but after that, he wouldn't have been afraid to make his interest known.

No, he was just glad he'd only referred to Ken as his babysitter. That he hadn't even hinted that he was only in Greenford because the government wanted him hidden.

Or that Alex wasn't even his real name.

"Just things," Alex said, waving off the question with a grunt. "What were you doing under the desk anyway?"

Cid glanced down, his expression almost sheepish. "Of all the things you could have tried to change the subject to."

Alex made as though to peer over the desk. "Why, is there something down there you shouldn't have? Or uh, *someone*?"

Cid shook his head. "There's no one out here but you and me. No, I was fiddling with the mini-fridge we have out here. Thing keeps making a weird sound, and it's been driving me crazy. Figured while no one was looking, I could take a look and uh, well, do something about it."

"And you're not supposed to do stuff like that," Alex guessed.

Cid scrunched up his nose. "I'm not allowed to do maintenance on things, especially electrical stuff. The first week I worked here, I tried getting a desk fan to work and electrocuted myself. So after that, it became a rule that I'm not allowed to fix anything."

Alex didn't know the man very well, but somehow, that story seemed to fit what he'd seen in their short interaction. There was no way in hell he would ever call the man inept or stupid. He didn't think it was possible to end up with a Ph.D. and be stupid. Yet there seemed something almost bumbling, in a charming way, about the other man. The sort of person he could see tripping over his own feet and end up the first person laughing after he'd hit the ground.

Cid straightened suddenly, eyes going wide. "Oh. Crap, right, you came in here."

"I did," Alex said, unable to help his amusement.

Cid muttered under his breath, then winced. "Sorry, I didn't even think about that. Sorry."

"It's fine," Alex assured him, a little bewildered.

Cid sighed. "I should have asked you what you came in for a long time ago. That's my fault. You caught me by surprise, then I realized who you were, and you distracted me."

"I distracted you, huh?" Alex asked with a smirk.

Cid flushed. "Yes. I got distracted and forgot...well, what should happen. Wait, you're a student here?"

"Would you be surprised if I was?" Alex asked.

Cid gave a laugh. "No, that's not what I meant at all!"

Alex grinned at that. Cid was a combination of mortified and amused, and it was a charming combination. It probably didn't help that Cid was just naturally boyish and good-looking, and Alex knew damn well that his own attraction to the man made plenty of what he did seem appealing.

"I just meant I haven't seen you around before, and I'm pretty sure I'd remember you," Cid told him.

"Is that so?" Alex asked in a low, interested voice.

Cid stared at him for a moment, blinking slowly. Then, with a shake of his head, he recovered and Alex couldn't help his pleased smirk. He'd long ago learned how to present himself to someone else to both get and hold their attention. From Cid's reaction, the slight color to his cheeks, the hard swallow that sent his Adam's Apple bobbing, and the nervous twitch of his fingers across the desk's surface, Alex could see he definitely had the man's attention, and all from a simple tonal change and a slight hint of something in his words.

"Yes," Cid said, clearing his throat and rallying impressively. "You're an easy person to notice in a crowd."

"And how's that?" Alex asked, a little curious.

"Other than your sheer size?"

"That sounds more like a compliment coming from you, not just something you've noticed," Alex said, making more of a guess than an actual observation on his own part.

"It could be," Cid said, watching Alex carefully now. "But your size is distinctive, your voice is deep and carries a good distance. You carry yourself with confidence, act with it too. You're also a little older than most of the students here. A lot of the students I see around here look like they just rolled out of high school, whereas you look like someone a little more...seasoned."

"Seasoned," Alex repeated. "I'm showing my age, huh?"

Cid chuckled. "I'd guess late twenties, *maybe* early thirties. It's about the time when I've noticed people's faces thin out, get a bit stronger in their features, but they aren't quite seeing the wear and tear that some people start to see in their later thirties all the way up to their late forties."

Alex was dutifully impressed by the assessment. Just a moment ago, he had been willing to think of Cid as a slightly bumbling but still intelligent man. Now he was beginning to see that the man had more skills than just his medical training. As much as his mind seemed to bounce and jitter all over the place, Cid was clearly picking up on facts, details, and patterns as we went along.

"Twenty-nine," Alex told him, thinking the tidbit of information was safe to admit.

Cid beamed at that. "Ooh, score one for me."

And just like that, Cid was completely laidback and

almost goofy again, as though a switch had been flipped. Alex realized that just a moment before, Cid had been clinical, precise, and utterly in the zone. Though he could only vaguely remember the scene on the street, Cid had been much the same then. The dichotomy was blatant now that Alex was seeing it, and he almost wanted to call it fascinating.

"So what are you studying?" Cid asked, cocking his head.

Alex snorted. "I'm not. I'm a janitor."

Cid blinked slowly, narrowing his eyes. "Oh. Well, damn, I had you pegged for a student after that conversation."

"Nope. Just clean the floors and wipe down the toilets," Alex said with a shrug.

Cid sighed. "Ah well, I guess my predictions can't be perfect, huh? Not perfect at all. Damn."

Alex snorted. "And just like that, all your interest flew out the window."

Cid looked up, brow furrowing. "Interest?"

For a moment, Alex genuinely couldn't tell if Cid was actually confused about Alex's meaning or if he was playing dumb to avoid admitting that he'd been even briefly interested in someone who scrubbed shit out of the inside of toilet bowls for a living. It wouldn't be the first time he'd ever seen someone from a far better way of life suddenly swerve when they realized they were dealing with one of *those* people.

"Oh!" Cid exclaimed suddenly, letting out a heavy laugh. "*Interest,* interest."

"Uh, yeah," Alex said slowly. "You being interested."

"In you," Cid added.

"Yeah."

"Well, that hasn't changed. Or…shit, hold on. Oh wait, I'm not supposed to swear, damn."

Alex couldn't help it, he tipped his head back and laughed. The sound filled the room, booming to every corner of the lobby. Watching this relative stranger stumble, fumble, and yet somehow manage to still navigate his way through the conversation with all the charm of an absolute dork was too much for him.

Cid put his face in his hands. "I swear, I *swear*, I'm not normally this awkward."

"Do you want to put that to the test?" Alex asked once he recovered enough breath to speak.

Cid looked up, his bright eyes glinting. "Is that a challenge?"

"Could be."

"Fine. I challenge you to a date."

It was Alex's turn to be taken off-guard, though he hoped he was at least marginally better at showing it. He didn't know what surprised him more, that Cid was willing to be so bold, or the fact that the man was actually asking for a date. Just a moment before, Alex had been convinced someone like Cid wouldn't be interested in the slightest thing from him.

"A date, huh?" Alex said, continuing the challenge.

Cid leaned forward, narrowing his eyes. "Yes, a date. Not a 'Grindr date' but a date, date. Food, drinks…actually, virgin drinks, considering what you just went through."

The last was added hastily, earning another grin from Alex.

Cid continued on. "You, me, a date."

"Bold strategy," Alex acknowledged. "But that would mean I want to go out on a date with you in the first place."

Cid's eyes narrowed further, darting over Alex's face. "I think you might."

"You sure?"

"No, but I'm still going to take the chance."

Alex had to admire the sort of confidence that came from plowing on despite the unknown. He had to admit there was something thrilling about the idea of a man who would blush and lose his thought at a growling tone of voice only moments before but was still willing to boldly push through and ask for a date.

It was stupid. It was foolish, he knew that. He wasn't even operating under his real name, let alone real history. Yet there was something about Cid's demeanor, bright and cheerful, that drew Alex in. Maybe he just needed a little bit of sunlight in his life, a pick-me-up that brought him out of the cloud he'd been living under ever since his world fell apart.

Or maybe it was just Cid.

Either way, he found himself chuckling. "Alright. Here's my number then."

Cid jotted it down, which amused Alex but he didn't comment on it when the man should have had his phone on hand. He wasn't going to question it, as he was sure it would probably be another story, although part of him wanted to know more.

"Now, let's actually talk about why you're here," Cid told him once he shoved the phone number into his pocket.

Alex grinned but told Cid what the problem was. Cid insisted upon a physical examination.

"Oh?" Alex asked in amusement.

Cid returned the smile. "Yes. Dr. Finn will look you over and get you sorted out. Just go through that door, and it'll be the second door on your left."

"Not getting your hands dirty yourself?" Alex asked, turning up a brow.

Cid smiled, bringing his attention back around to his computer. "I'm just a resident. Dr. Finn is on call today and I'm supposed to be manning the front. So she'll be the one to see you."

"You're missing out," Alex told him, going for the door.

"Or, depending on how our date goes, I'm awaiting the inevitable," Cid called back to him.

Alex chuckled at that, opening the door and leaving the man behind to enter a long hallway of doors. It was then that his head twinged, bringing a wince. It was also the point where he realized that his general feeling of sickness and the pain in his head hadn't bothered him the whole time he'd been talking to Cid.

CID

It ended up being a couple more days before Cid could actually use the phone number he'd been given. His new phone had finally shown up at his home on Tuesday, and after getting it started up and transferring everything he could salvage from the old phone, he finally dug out the number he'd tucked away in a desk drawer.

Hey, he typed out. *It's Cid. Sorry it took me a bit to message you, but my old phone was broken, so I had to wait for this one to show up.*

Happy with the text, he shoved his new phone into his pocket, grabbed his gym bag and left. There was no reply by the time he reached the campus or by the time he'd jogged to the university's gym. Rather than letting himself get too focused on his phone, he plugged his headphones into it, set his music blasting and focused on his workout.

He'd never been all that big on building muscle, though aesthetically speaking, Cid enjoyed at least a little bulk on his body. Instead, he was fond of cardio and could have happily spent hours on a treadmill or on the indoor track. Perhaps, if his home life had been more stable, he might have been able to join a track team, but he'd moved around a little too often for that.

By the time a couple of hours had passed, he found himself finally looking at his phone. His heart skipped a couple of beats as he saw he had a text message from Alex.

Not surprised ya did somethin with ur old one, sounds like u

Cid laughed softly. Apparently, the man already had a good feel for Cid.

Yeah, I had an accident.

So u textin 2 do that date?

That I am. Still up for it?

There was a pause in the conversation then, and Cid realized he was jiggling his leg nervously. He had been the one to ask for the date in the first place, and that would have been the prime time to be nervous. Apparently, his nerves had a few days to marinate in his skull and were doing their best to creep up on him now that he had to wait and see if Alex was as committed to the date as Cid was.

Yea, when?

Cid grinned and began happily typing back. After that, it was only a matter of setting up the time and place for them to meet. He knew he was grinning like an idiot by the time they left the conversation, but he didn't care one bit as he shoved his phone back into his pocket.

Only for it to then immediately buzz, this time with a message from Alice.

Where are you?

The gym.

Of course you are. Meet me out front in five?

Make it ten, I want to rinse off and change.

Ten it is.

Tucking his phone away once more, he jogged over to

the locker rooms to quickly rinse himself off and change back into normal clothes. With his hair still wet from the quick shower, he joined Alice outside as she leaned against one of the trees, a cigarette held between her fingers.

"You know the campus is smoke-free, right?" Cid asked her.

Alice looked over, taking an inhale from her cigarette. "I'm not smoking around anyone else. I'm being courteous."

"You're also smoking outside the building devoted to health and safety," Cid pointed out, adjusting the strap of his gym bag so it sat comfortably on his shoulder.

Alice shrugged. "Consider me a warning to everyone else. The hazards of being a dirty, filthy smoker."

"It is pretty gross," Cid pointed out with a wrinkle of his nose.

"It is," she admitted. "I almost quit this past winter too."

"You said that about the one before."

"Smoking in the winter sucks, okay?"

"Smoking in general sucks."

"Thanks, Doc," she told him, rolling her eyes. "I was hoping we could grab a coffee at the cafe across from the campus. That is if you're done lecturing me."

"Only giving helpful, valid medical advice," Cid said with a grin.

"Sure you are," she muttered, putting out the cigarette and tossing the butt into the nearby trash can. "And why are you so perky?"

"I'm always perky," Cid told her as they began to walk. "It's something you've said is my most charming feature."

"I said it *can* be charming," Alice corrected. "But not when I've had the unfortunate luck to deal with you after I've just woken up."

"Hey, I hadn't been awake very long either!" Cid protested.

"Which is precisely what makes the entire thing even more horrifying. Who the hell wakes up with a smile on their face? Weird people, that's who."

"You've already told me several times in the past week that I'm weird, so that should be a given."

"Yes, but you don't have to look so smug about it."

Cid let out a laugh, bumping her lightly with his shoulder. Alice could be so serious and somewhat grumpy, but he wasn't fooled by it. There was mischief in the woman that he'd always appreciated, and if you were willing to be gently bullied from time to time, she had a wicked sense of humor. And honestly, despite how much she teased him or complained about his happy demeanor, Cid was almost a hundred percent sure she loved it.

"No, but really, what's got you in such a good mood?" she asked.

"I might or might not have a date Friday night," Cid said, not caring that he was beaming.

"No shit!" she exclaimed. "Is that what you've been going to the gym for? Picking up some sweaty jock?"

Cid chuckled. "No. Uh, you remember that guy from the other night?"

"Which night and which guy?"

"The one we found outside the strip club."

Alice screwed up her eyes in thought and then gave a heavy snort. "Please tell me you aren't going on a date with him."

"What's wrong with that?" Cid asked.

"I mean, you guy's first met when he was literally puking on the sidewalk."

"It's not his fault he was drugged."

"So, he confirmed that?"

"He did."

There was a flicker of doubt in her eyes but she shrugged. "Alright."

"Plus, your first introduction to me wasn't all that great. And now look at us."

That brought a laugh from the woman. "I still say you ruptured something in me when your big ass landed on me."

"I did not," Cid frowned. "I checked and everything."

It had been the previous autumn when he'd first come to Greenford to start his residency at the clinic. Feeling a little lonely and a lot bored, he'd decided to go to the faculty Halloween party. It had rained heavily throughout the day, and the entire campus was soaked through and completely covered in mud.

Which had included the stairs he'd tried to climb two at a time. He hadn't been paying attention to where he was going and had almost managed to avoid barreling into Alice as she reached the next landing. He would have done it too, if it wasn't for a smear of mud on the step that sent his attempted pivot into a full lunge forward. He'd ended up glad there was a landing there in the first place to catch them. Otherwise, it could have been a lot worse.

Not the most graceful of introductions, but it had somehow worked for them.

"Well, at least I can say the party wasn't boring," Alice said, shaking her head.

"See. I have my uses," Cid told her with a smile.

She eyed him. "And please tell me you're not going out for drinks. I think he's probably seen enough alcohol to last him for a couple of months at least."

Cid snorted. "Yeah, I had the same thought. Wasn't too

sure what to do since there's not a lot of...well, anything here."

"There's plenty to do here if you think hard enough," Alice told him as they reached the edge of the campus. "Hell, just get some food and walk around town. The weather is supposed to be great this whole week. I'm sure you guys can just walk and talk."

"True," Cid admitted, thinking that wasn't a bad idea.

"Or just find a nice secluded spot and have your way with him," Alice added as they stepped off the campus line.

"I'm not..." Cid began, letting out a laugh, "going on a date to get laid."

"Isn't that the point of dates?"

"I thought the point of dates was to check if you were compatible with someone."

"Sex is a type of compatibility."

Cid rolled his eyes, knowing she was intentionally trying to bait him. "For *more* than just that."

Not that he was against the idea. There was absolutely no question in his mind about whether or not he'd be willing to sleep with Alex if given the chance. There was something rough about the other man, but Cid detected warmth under the man's easy smirk and dry delivery. It was only a gut instinct but Cid had learned to listen to those instincts.

"You're thinking about him naked right now, aren't you?" Alice asked wryly.

"No," Cid said, though his thoughts had certainly been heading in that direction.

"You know, if he *does* turn out to be trouble, you probably shouldn't sleep with him."

"If everyone followed that rule, you'd never get laid."

She swatted him even as she laughed. "That's not the conversation we're having right now, you little shit."

"And what happens if I find out he's trouble *after* I sleep with him?"

"Well, then you'll just have to deal with it. Lord knows I hope it's worth it."

"You're awfully pessimistic. Has anyone ever told you that?"

Alice shrugged. "I just don't like nasty surprises, is all. And I don't want you to be the one to receive one."

"C'mon, at least let me spend some time with him before you condemn him."

"You're allowed to date whoever you want, even if I don't think it's a good idea."

Cid sighed, shaking his head. Maybe he wasn't being as cautious as she believed he should be, but he didn't see the point in letting one messy introduction get in the way of something that, at the very least, could be fun. And if it happened to lead to something more meaningful, all the better.

"Let's go get hopped up on caffeine and sugar," Alice told him, opening the cafe door to the rich scent of coffee. "And then you can tell me how the hell you even ran into the guy again in the first place."

ALEX

It was only as Friday grew later that Alex realized he didn't really have a whole lot in the way of clothes to choose from. All his clothes were plain long sleeve shirts, jackets, and jeans. It wasn't like he needed anything else. Living in Greenford while under protection was meant to keep him not only under the radar but give him some sense of freedom.

Admittedly, freedom that still came with a leash attached. When Ken had called earlier in the week, he had not been happy to find out Alex had been temporarily hospitalized. The false name they had him living under worked just fine, raising zero suspicion, but he hadn't been happy that no one had been alerted when Alex had been checked in.

That, of course, had started a whole conversation about whether or not Alex might need to be relocated again, something neither Alex nor Ken wanted. Alex was growing quite fond of the sleepy and somewhat quirky little town, and he didn't want to start all over. For Ken's part, that would require even more investment in keeping Alex in one piece, and Alex guessed budget was a hot topic.

In the end, Alex had settled on promising not to go to crowded clubs anymore. He'd had to argue to be able to go to restaurants at night and then bars, but only if they weren't packed. Alex could feel the leash getting a little shorter, but it still hadn't gone tight, so he would live with it. Yet, he hadn't mentioned his upcoming date, the one that had him annoyed as he stared at his array of bland clothes.

"Oh fuck it," he muttered, grabbing the red long sleeve that he never wore. "It's not like this is some fancy shit."

He probably should have never agreed to go on the date in the first place. What exactly was he expecting to happen? Hell, Alex hadn't been on a date since his early twenties, having learned that it was far easier and probably safer to keep himself single. And now, all of a sudden, he thought it was a great idea while he was living under an assumed name, in some town he'd probably never see again after his federal protection was no longer needed.

That only served to make him roll his eyes as he pulled on his clothes. His only motivation for trying to live somewhat independently was to have something of a life. It wouldn't be much of a life if he just went to work, occasionally had a drink, and stayed in his one-bedroom apartment that was adorned with the most basic, flimsy furniture that was probably bought wholesale.

Greenford was a perfect excuse for him to live a life that didn't circle around the Los Muertos anymore. Back in Port Dale, he'd constantly had to be on alert and ready for when they might want him for *something*. Even if he didn't do a lot of the dirty work, there were always little jobs laying around for him to be thrown at, and he would have done whatever it took to keep his brother from being pulled into the mess.

If he was going to pretend to have a normal life, then going on dates was a great way to do that. The fact that he hadn't been on a date in years was a good enough reason for him to go out with Cid. And the fact that he'd never truly been comfortable enough to go on a date with another guy before, due to always have to make sure no one from the gang saw him, was another good reason to go.

And hell, the guy was cute, and he had a nice smile, which was more than enough even without the other two reasons.

———

"HEY," Cid called as he jogged up to meet Alex on the sidewalk. "Am I late?"

"Naw, I'm just early," Alex admitted.

It seemed he wasn't the only one who had decided to go with a long-sleeved shirt. Though Cid's was bright blue, a compliment to his lighter skin and his bright eyes. It also had a low collar, showing off his collarbones. Alex wasn't sure if it was a sign of how long it had been since he'd last got laid or how attractive he found Cid, but he had a strong urge to nibble on them.

"Well, that's good, that's good," Cid said, eyes darting around. "I uh, gotta admit, I didn't actually have a plan for tonight. I meant to think about it more, but then I kinda didn't..."

Alex chuckled. "I mean, it's a date, right? How hard can they be?"

"I didn't really get a lot of time for dating in med

school," Cid admitted sheepishly. "So I'm a little rusty on dates."

"Well, my last date was like...ten years ago," Alex told him with a shrug. "And it was with a woman. So I'm not doing any better."

"A woman, huh?" Cid asked curiously. "Were you still in the closet then or..."

"Well, I used to pretty much not talk about the fact that I was into guys," Alex explained. "People I used to know wouldn't have been very happy to know I liked dudes."

"Oh," Cid said with a frown. "Well, I'm glad you don't have to be around those people anymore."

"Yeah, you and me both," Alex muttered. "Though I'm sure they'd like to see me again."

"Really? Sounds like they weren't all that great," Cid said.

Alex cursed himself inwardly. "They weren't...and aren't. And they're not happy with me, so probably good I don't see 'em again."

He waited for the inevitable questions that were sure to follow. There was enough vagueness and mystery in his words to prompt any normal person's curiosity. Alex was desperately trying to figure out what he could say to the other man to keep him from prying too closely while also not being belligerently evasive at the same time.

Cid sidled up next to him, bumping him with his hip. "So, how do you feel about yogurt?"

Alex looked up, hesitating as the unexpected question took a moment to process through his thoughts. "Yogurt?"

"Yeah, you know, dairy product usually has fruit involved, sometimes granola. Jamie Lee Curtis was the face of the brand that helps you poop. Yogurt."

Alex let out a surprised bark of laughter. "I know what yogurt is, you ass."

"Right, so, how do you feel about it."

"Last I checked, it's yogurt."

Cid rolled his eyes, but the corner of his mouth twitched, tempting Alex to plant his lips on him. "I deserved that. But I mean, do you hate yogurt?"

"I don't have strong feelings about yogurt."

"How about the frozen kind?"

"Never had it."

Cid's eyes lit up. "Really? Well, then I have the place I'm dragging you to. Easy."

Alex eyed him. "Dragging me, huh?"

"Yeah, you have no choice whatsoever. We're getting frozen yogurt and you're going to love it."

"Is that a bet?"

"Damn right."

DAMN IT, the frozen yogurt *was* good.

Alex had been a little doubtful about the cramped, poorly lit random store that seemed shoved in between a liquor store and a laundromat. Yet the selection had been varied enough to attract his attention, and the items themselves were brightly lit in the freezers.

Alex had gone with coconut flavor and chose to go without any sort of toppings or mixings. Cid had gone the whole hog, getting a lime frozen yogurt with an assortment of berries and some pieces of chocolate sprinkled on top. At the first wary taste, Alex's eyes had widened as they'd stepped back onto the street.

"Alright, you win," Alex admitted as he shoved another spoonful onto his tongue.

"Good?" Cid asked, bright eyes watching Alex.

"When I was growing up," Alex told him as they began to walk side by side. "There was this little store on the corner over from our apartment building. I mean, it wasn't much, just a shitty hole in the wall, but they had some food too. The owners made it all, the wife liked to make ice cream and one of my favorites was this coconut flavored one she did. This reminds me of that. My brother liked lime or lemon...though he'd go for something else sometimes too."

"You have a brother?" Cid asked, taking a bite of his own yogurt.

"Had," Alex said softly.

A pang shot through him at that one simple word. Rio, who should have been alive. Rio, who should be the one standing on a street corner, seeing how positively green and alive Greenford really was, free from the stress, combat, and near-death of living in Port Dale, was not there at all.

And never would be.

"What was his favorite flavor?" Cid asked.

Alex glanced at him as Cid licked another spoonful of frozen yogurt from his spoon. Alex couldn't figure out if Cid was being dense or intentionally avoiding the subject that Alex had dropped on him. Whatever the case, he was thankful to have the reprieve from the memories that threatened to wrap around him and bring him down.

Alex eyed Cid's cup. "Lime. Like yours."

"A man of fine taste, I say," Cid said, taking another lick.

"We didn't have a whole lot," Alex said, giving a heavy shrug. "Grew up in a shitty part of town. But every once in a while, I could get some change together and treat us to some ice cream and maybe a little taco or something. It wasn't much."

Cid chuckled. "Sometimes it's the little things that matter the most to people."

Alex frowned in thought, privately hoping that was the case. His brother had never seemed unhappy, but that was just Rio's nature. He had always been the one to make Alex smile or drag a laugh out of him. When their mother had forgotten to pay the utilities, both he and Rio had been left in a dark apartment in the middle of winter. It had been Rio who'd kept their spirits up, refusing to let Alex's dark mood get the better of him. And in turn, it had been Alex who had found a way to get the money together to get everything turned back on again.

It was the first time he'd ever had to suck it up and do something for Los Muertos.

"My parents died when I was six," Cid told him.

Alex looked up, a little startled. "Oh. Shit. I'm sorry to hear that."

Cid shook his head, still smiling. "It's okay. Like I said, I was six, so I don't really remember them all that much. But I do have this one memory. It's pretty strong. I guess we didn't have a whole lot of money, so doing stuff as a family was pretty limited. But I remember going to the park one time and being able to run around like a little idiot for a few hours. It was a scorching hot day, and I almost passed out until my dad made me stop and get some water from a fountain and cool down."

"Sounds like slowing down is a problem for you," Alex observed.

Cid laughed. "Yeah. But while I was resting, losing my mind the whole time because I wanted to be running around, my mom came back. She had this little cup of frozen yogurt that she'd grabbed. I don't know if they just didn't want some, or they didn't want to spend the money on themselves, but they didn't have one. So I sat there, under a tree with my parents, eating that yogurt and giving them bites."

They had cleared the busier parts of the city and drifted toward one of the many little parks that were dotted around the city. In a town that embraced its very green and natural surroundings, the people, either planned or simply by accident, had allowed spaces around the city where the grass was only trimmed, the trees were left untouched, and occasionally someone would set down a picnic table or maybe a set of swings and a slide.

The two of them had unconsciously drifted into one of those places, with just the two of them stepping onto the grass.

"That sounds really sweet," Alex said, meaning it. "And I'm guessing that's why you're so fond of it as an adult."

Cid grinned down at his almost empty cup of frozen yogurt. "Yeah, it reminds me of that day, well, and it's delicious too. But that's what I mean, those little things can be not so little to other people."

"How nosy would it be to ask what happened to you after that?" Alex asked.

Cid shook his head, reaching up to run his hand through a low hanging branch. "It wouldn't be nosy, I think anyone would wonder. Nothing too exciting happened, though. We didn't have any other family to help, so I ended up being put into the foster care system."

"Ouch," Alex muttered. "That had to suck."

It was the exact fate that Alex had worried about for himself, and then for Rio after Alex reached eighteen. All it would have taken was one well-meaning person to call child protective services and Rio would have quickly been taken away from the apartment. Their mother wasn't exactly subtle in her drug addiction, and as far as the government was concerned, Alex didn't have a job. Not only would that have resulted in the brothers being separated, but Alex had heard the stories of kids who'd gone through the system and he didn't want that for his younger brother.

Again, Cid shook his head. "It wasn't so bad. Sure, sometimes you got placed in a house where it was obvious the people did the bare minimum to keep the checks coming, or maybe to brag to their friends about fostering. But most people were just...people, doing their best with what they had. I keep in contact with a couple of the houses I went to, nothing like super close or anything but I touch base, see how they're doing, tell them how I'm doing."

"I've heard some things," Alex said slowly as they stepped around a tree in their path, Cid once more playing with the leaves on a branch.

"Eh, you hear a lot of things, and I know some of the other kids I met had some things happen that uh, well, yeah. Maybe I just got lucky? All I know is, I don't have any horror stories. Sure it got a little lonely at times, and getting moved around randomly wasn't the best, but I think I did pretty good for myself," Cid explained, this time running his hand down the trunk of a tree.

Alex wasn't sure that was the description he would have used. Being pushed through different houses, never knowing where you were going to go, or what the people there would be like had to have been exhausting and depressing. Yet not one drop of darkness seemed to have touched Cid in the slightest, who seemed perfectly happy to have himself a cup of frozen yogurt while walking through the trees.

"I think you did more than pretty good," Alex told him.

Cid beamed at him. "Thank you, Alex."

There was a slight twinge of guilt at that. While it was obvious the two of them were enjoying each other, he hated that he was still operating under false pretenses. There was only so much he could tell the other man about himself, and Alex was going to have to either decide to lie or find some other solution to keep Cid from digging too deeply. The man had been pretty understanding and tolerant so far, but if they continued to see one another more, Alex couldn't see that patience being unlimited.

"Eh," Alex said, looking away. "Just speaking the truth."

"Oh, I see," Cid said and Alex could hear the smile in his voice.

Alex rolled his eyes, tugging the sleeves of his shirt up to his elbows with a jerk of his hands. He had never been fond of long sleeves, they always ended up bunching up around his wrists, got caught on things more often, and unless it was the dead of winter in Port Dale, it was usually just a way to bake yourself alive in the sun.

"I'm glad you see," Alex grunted.

"So, where are you from?" Cid asked.

Alex looked up, raising a brow. "What makes you think I'm not from around here?"

"Uhh, well," Cid began, face beginning to color again. "Well...you don't look like the other people I've seen around here who're lifers."

Alex watched the other man as his eyes darted up and down him, but they kept coming to rest on his arms. Alex looked down, sighing as he realized that both of his forearms had been bared and the tattoos he kept hidden from most people were on full display in the light of the lowering sun.

"Why, because I look like a thug?" Alex guessed.

Cid's color remained but his nervous expression was replaced by a frown. "I don't think you look like a thug. Why would you say that?"

Alex shrugged, absently running a hand over his tattooed arm. "You wouldn't be the first person to think it."

Cid sighed. "Well, I don't. I don't care that you're a janitor, and I don't care that you're stupidly tall, ridiculously buff, and are covered in tattoos."

"Stupidly tall?"

"Plus, I like that."

"My being stupidly tall?"

"And everything else I said too."

"So you like thugs?"

Cid tried to glare at him in response, but Alex wasn't sure he could actually manage so dour an expression. If anything, it made the man look somehow even more endearing, if a little bit like he was pouting. It wasn't helped by the fact that Alex could see the corners of Cid's mouth were twitching in response.

"I think I like *you*," Cid said instead of arguing further.

Alex had been prepared for an honest attempt at refuting what he'd said or for Cid to make some sort of quip. He was thrown off a little by the blatant and honest expression of attraction and one that didn't focus on his ass or his arms.

"We barely know each other," Alex pointed out.

Cid laughed, reaching down between them to take Alex's hand in his. "Isn't that the point of going on dates? To see if you like each other and get to know one another?"

"Dates?" Alex asked, attention honing in on the feel of Cid's nimble fingers curling around his own blunter ones. "As in plural?"

"Yeah," Cid said, turning to look up at the sky. "I think

I'd like to see if I could like you even more as I learn more. What do you say?"

"I," Alex began, clearing his throat. "Sure. Yeah."

Cid didn't seem bothered by Alex's less than enthusiastic response. In truth, Alex had no idea how he was supposed to respond. He really wasn't used to people liking him at their first meeting, though he supposed he shouldn't be surprised that Cid would break the mold when the guy had still wanted a first date after finding Alex puking in the streets.

"Great," Cid beamed. "So how would you feel about finishing up our date by being super cheesy and watching the sun go down together?"

Alex huffed out a soft laugh. "Yeah, Cid, we can do that."

CID

After a series of taps on the tablet, Cid looked up to the frail-looking young man sitting on the examination table. The freshman had come in an hour before, complaining of a constantly upset stomach, a headache, nightmares, and a whole host of other problems.

"So?" the young man, Jeremy, finally spit out. "How bad is it?"

Cid gave him a warm smile. "Well, based on the little conversation we just had, I'd say that it's not that bad at all."

"Really? I can't sleep half the time."

"I know. So what I'm going to prescribe is that you drop one of your classes while you still have the time to do it. After that, I'd advise going to some social events or calling up a couple of friends and doing something online with them. Also, I hear great things about meditation and possibly therapy," Cid said, tapping in the last bit of information.

Jeremy straightened. "What?"

"It's stress," Cid told him gently. "You're not the first case of stress-related illness that's walked through these doors. You've taken a lot on your plate, and that sort of stress is awful on your system. This is your body telling you to take it easy. So, one less class for less stress, some fun to relieve stress, meditation because of the overall benefits, and therapy because stress can affect the way your brain works in the long term if you're exposed to it for too long and a professional can help."

"You're telling me this is *stress*?" the young man asked incredulously.

"Happens all the time," Cid told him with a smile. "Trust me, I had a bit of that when I was going through med school. You just need to dial back what you can and relax when you need it. Trust me, try it out, and if that doesn't work, come back in and we can see what we can do for you."

"I'd still feel better if we like...ran tests or something. Just to make sure it's not something serious," Jeremy muttered, picking at the paper on the table.

"Well, we can do that if you'd like," Cid said. He didn't think it was necessary, as Jeremy was not the first nor would he be the last student to show up in the clinic showing clear signs of stress-induced symptoms. "Hope you're not afraid of needles."

Jeremy shook his head. "No, I got a tattoo last month. I think I'll be alright."

Cid chuckled as he opened the door. "You say that, but we've had people with tattoos *and* piercings come in here and practically faint at the sight of a medical needle. I'll have someone come in and draw your blood, and you can set up an appointment at the desk to come in for the results. Oh, and I would still take my advice in the meantime, just to try it out, okay?"

"I think I can do that," Jeremy said, then frowning.

"Don't know about the class thing, though. Pretty sure my parents would blow a gasket if I dropped a class."

"Better they be unhappy about it than have their son's health deteriorate to a dangerous point," Cid pointed out, leaving Jeremy to think on it.

The electronic system took care of filing away his notes from the examination and he tucked the little tablet into the pocket of his coat as he stepped out into the lobby once more. The other two doctors were also on staff, which meant Cid wasn't necessarily needed out the front, but sometimes finding students to fill the role as receptionist could be a hit or miss sort of thing. So until they found a suitable replacement, again, he would have to play two roles.

He'd just sat down when Dr. Finn emerged from the hallway, looking down at her own device. "Blood tests? I'd say it was simple stress."

Cid chuckled. "Simple stress, she says, as if there's anything simple about it."

"Oh, I remember my college days all too well," she told him wryly.

Cid shrugged. "He insisted. I told him what I thought it was, based on the information, but he wanted to get more testing done. His insurance company isn't going to throw a fit over a few standard blood tests, especially because it *could* be something hormonal or an imbalance the tests could pick up. Plus, again, the patient specifically requested it."

It would have been one thing if the guy had asked for an ultra-expensive test that was unnecessary. Then, Cid would have explained that unless there's a strong case behind it, insurance companies were not going to fork over for it. But for something as standard as a few blood tests? He didn't see any reason to argue, especially if he was right and the blood tests came back normal and gave poor Jeremy some peace of mind.

"I see you really picked up on the whole patient advocacy thing during med school," Dr. Finn noted, finally closing down her tablet.

"That sounds suspiciously like a compliment coming from you, Dr. Finn," Cid said with a grin.

"Your suspicions are correct," she said with a slow smile. "And since I have you here, rumor is, you found yourself a date sometime this week."

Cid blinked. "How the hell did you find out about that?"

"I have my ways," Dr. Finn said mysteriously.

"That or Alice came in here looking for me at some point and the two of you started gossiping again," Cid accused. "Don't think I don't know about you two being in cahoots."

"You make us sound so diabolical."

While he wouldn't go *that* far, he certainly wouldn't say that it didn't cause him a little bit of worry. The two of them had met shortly after the Halloween party debacle when Alice had come in to grab Cid for a quick lunch. The two women had hit it off immediately, and they were not shy about comparing notes and then coming to Cid later.

"Is this where you two start getting nosy and interfering again?" Cid asked suspiciously.

"No," Dr. Finn turned to look at him with a raised brow. "Why, is there something I should be interfering over?"

"No," Cid told her. "It was a date. There's no need to get worried. No matter what Alice might have said."

"She only told me that you found yourself a date," Dr. Finn told him, sitting on the edge of the desk. "Though now

I'm quite curious what she might have said that has you so concerned."

Cid groaned and knew there was no way he was getting out of telling her now. With a heavy sigh, he regaled the story of when they had found Alex, ill and almost completely out of it on the street. He then had to mention that Alex had come into the clinic, and that was when Cid had the bright idea for a date.

"Huh," Dr. Finn said once he was done. "Well, I honestly don't see what the cause for concern is. It sounds like a perfectly fine way to meet someone."

"Really?" Cid asked doubtfully.

Dr. Finn chuckled. "No, it's a peculiar way, but I think that makes it all the more charming."

"I think Alice is just worried because she's not totally sold on the idea that he'd been drugged," Cid grumbled.

"Ah, well, that's Alice. She's the first to see a shadow, which means she might see one where there isn't. But since you're here and seem perfectly happy and talking about this Alex in the present tense, I'm guessing your date with him went well?"

Cid grinned. "Yeah, it really did."

It had been a little strange at first, and not just because it was the first date he'd had in a little while. It was obvious to Cid that Alex was keeping something close to his chest, though Cid couldn't begin to guess what it was. Still, Cid wasn't going to push the man, especially when they barely knew one another. If Alex was keeping something to himself, it was probably for a good reason and Cid didn't have any reason to suspect the man of anything.

"So what'd you do?" Dr. Finn asked, leaning in.

"Nothing like *that*," Cid told her, sensing the curiosity

on her part was coming from a less than wholesome place. "All clothes stayed on."

Well, except for the sleeves of Alex's shirt, baring what Cid was pretty sure was only half if not less than what was probably on the rest of Alex. He thought he'd done a pretty good job of playing it cool, but there had been a rush of interest and lust when he'd spotted the tattoos. Maybe Alice was right, and he just had a thing for the bad boy look, but he didn't think that was necessarily a bad thing because it didn't have to mean that Alex was bad.

Dr. Finn snorted, waving him off. "I know, I know, you're a good boy who doesn't put out on the first date."

"Right. Yeah. Totally," Cid said, looking away.

"Or you do and you just behaved yourself this time," Dr. Finn corrected, now smirking.

"We had a nice time," Cid insisted, refusing to add any more details that the woman might be looking for. "Got some frozen yogurt, walked around town, and we talked."

"Oh. A very tame, casual sort of thing then."

"Yeah, I mean, neither of us have really done a whole lot of dating. And I'm not a big believer in flashy first dates."

"They are rather hard to top."

"Exactly. And big, flashy dates always made me feel like you'd just be paying attention to what's happening on the date instead of, you know, the person you're on a date with. You're supposed to get to know people on a date, not be overwhelmed because you're at some fancy restaurant, or trying to keep a firm grip because they took you rock climbing."

Dr. Finn laughed. "I'll have you know that's how I met my last girlfriend."

"Yeah, but you were already rock climbing. So that was

a thing for you both. I'd need a new pair of pants if someone did that to me," Cid complained.

"What a charming thought," Dr. Finn said with a low snort.

"I'm chock full of charm," Cid told her. "And also absolutely terrified of climbing up a sheer rock wall with only a bit of rope to keep me from splatting on the ground."

They both looked up when the soft chime of the front door went off. Cid straightened when he saw the familiar face of Alex walking in, glancing around as he went. Cid noticed then that Alex tended to walk with his shoulders hunched as though he was ready to charge forward at a moment's notice. It gave him a swagger, and Cid smiled as he drew closer, dark eyes falling on Cid's face.

"Hello," Dr. Finn greeted cheerfully, sliding off the desk smoothly to stand upright. "Walk-in or appointment?"

"A walk-in to maybe make an appointment," Alex told her in his deep, rumbling voice.

"Well, howdy stranger," Cid said, grinning.

"Hey," Alex said, stopping once he reached the desk. "I just finished my shift. Figured I'd stop in and see if you were around."

"Well, here I am," Cid told him.

"Oh," Dr. Finn said, looking Alex over. "This must be our mystery man."

Alex's brow furrowed. "Mystery man?"

Cid rolled his eyes. "She's being facetious. There's no mystery whatsoever, but my friends are a bunch of gossips and troublemakers. I promise you I was completely honest with them about Friday night."

Though from the way Dr. Finn's eyes glanced over Alex when he wasn't looking, Cid thought maybe he hadn't done the man enough justice in his physical description of him.

Cid scowled at her over Alex's shoulder when her eyes met his, and with a soft laugh she waved him off, walking back toward the hallway once more.

"You've got about twenty minutes until you'll have to finish up with Jeremy," Dr. Finn told him before disappearing.

"Jeremy?" Alex asked.

"Patient we have in at the moment," Cid explained. "So, what brings you in here? Not that I'm complaining, you did manage to save me from being interrogated further."

Alex cocked his head. "From your friend?"

"And my boss. Who just so happens to take a strong interest in my personal life. I haven't quite been able to decide if that's a good thing or not."

"Really glad I don't have that relationship with my boss. I don't know what I'd do if Archy started asking after my personal business. Shit, I think he's still not totally convinced I'm not wasted when I come into work."

Cid frowned at that. "I guess you weren't kidding about people judging you pretty hard sometimes."

Alex shrugged his wide shoulders. "You get used to it. Plus, it's not like I'm exactly free from sin anyway."

Once more, Cid found himself sensing there was more to the story than Alex was sharing with him. Yet once again, he held his tongue, believing that if Alex wanted to tell him, he would in his own time. They barely knew one another, and Cid didn't want to put the man through a barrage of questions he wasn't quite ready to answer yet.

So he went with the far easier one. "So, what brings you in here?"

"I already said," Alex said with a frown.

Cid thought about that for a moment and then let out a laugh. "Oh! Was that 'walk in' comment about me?"

"Yeah."

Cid didn't bother to hide his delight. "You want to go on another date?"

"Well, I was actually gonna ask when you usually have lunch. Figured we could go somewhere nearby and grab something to eat. Then, I don't know, figured we could have a chill night or something. Not go anywhere but just watch movies or something."

"Are you inviting me to your house?" Cid asked with a wry grin.

"If ya want, yeah. My apartment ain't exactly special, though," Alex warned him.

It was the first time Cid thought he'd ever noticed a hint of something almost like embarrassment from the other man. Cid really didn't care if Alex's place wasn't all that fancy, but he was beginning to sense that maybe the other man was a little more bothered by their different lifestyles.

"Well, there's a couple of places just off campus and I can generally snag an hour for lunch whenever I want," Cid told him. "So anytime tomorrow would be great for me. And really, if you want, you can come over to my place. Might as well get more use out of my sound system than I already do."

Alex considered that for a moment then nodded. "Alright. That works out just fine for me."

"Great," Cid said with a smile. "Friday again?"

"Yeah. I work a little bit later that day, so meet you at your place at like...eight?"

"Eight works for me."

Alex shook his head. "You're always smiling, ya know that?"

"I've been told it's a thing that I do," Cid admitted.

Alex snorted, turning to walk away. "I'll see you

tomorrow when I go on lunch."

"See you then," Cid said, waving at his back.

He was not at all surprised to hear the hallway door open once again when the front door stopped chiming. Dr. Finn peered out carefully, then caught sight of Cid who was ignoring her and watching Alex leave the building.

"Damn," Dr. Finn muttered. "Where did you say you found him again? Were there more like him wandering around?"

Cid laughed. "No, just him. And considering how I found him, maybe you shouldn't go looking either."

"That man looks like he could break me in half with just one hand," she muttered.

"I know," Cid said with a grin. "It's pretty great, isn't it?"

Yeah, he had a type, and he was perfectly okay with that.

Dr. Finn smirked. "And I'm pretty sure you're on your way to wrapping him around your little finger."

Cid laughed at that. "You're reading more into this than I am. I can barely read his face most of the time."

"He's just got one of those super-serious faces and prob-ably takes himself a little too seriously," Dr. Finn explained. "My dad was like that, but you learn to read them fast enough."

"Oh, teach me the ways," Cid said with an air of wist-fulness.

"If you stop being a smart ass, I might," Dr. Finn told him.

"You're going to ask me to repeat the story about our date again, aren't you?" Cid realized.

"Damn right," she said, plopping down on the desk again. "Now get to it.

ALEX

He wouldn't have admitted it aloud, but Alex had found himself thinking about the lunch he had agreed to. Well, not just agreed to but had actively suggested.

It was a little strange for him, but Alex had to privately admit that he'd had Cid on his mind ever since their first date. The man had just been a bright ball of sunshine and energy, possessing both childlike joy and the wisdom and patience of someone far older. It was weird to think of someone he barely knew so fondly, but it had been a genuine pleasure to spend time with Cid. Just those couple of hours together had brightened the rest of Alex's night and had crept into his thoughts in the days after.

"Hey, Archy," he called as he popped his head into the classroom his supervisor was mopping. "I'm going to take my lunch."

Archy grunted, waving him off without a word. Alex took that as acknowledgment and permission and slipped back out into the hallway. The guy who should have been helping clean up the art and history building had called in, so Archy had been helping him for most of the day. Funnily, Alex preferred the older man's company to most of the other people he worked with. Archy wasn't exactly big on talking, but he knew his stuff, and his willingness to get his hands dirty to keep the workflow smooth only served to earn Alex's respect.

And he thought the older man was starting to grow fond of him.

He'd already texted Cid to let him know he was getting ready to take his lunch to give the man a chance to either delay or cancel it if he wanted. Cid had responded quite enthusiastically and with many happy emojis thrown into the message as well. Alex didn't think he'd ever met someone who was unabashedly earnest before, showcasing his interest with doubt or hesitation.

He was also beginning to wonder if maybe that was a weakness of his because he was liking such bald interest from another person.

When he stepped out of the building, he found himself bathed in sunlight. He squinted up to the sky, finding only a few light, fluffy clouds hanging in the backdrop of the bright, blue sky. Alex could easily picture that this was the sort of weather Cid probably adored, and he was glad it had cleared up from the gray overcast sky he'd seen in the morning.

They'd agreed to meet near the main administration building, located near the front of the campus. It took Alex only about five minutes to get there from where he was and he found the campus relatively empty of traffic. It was about the right time for most of the classes to still be in session, but he figured that by the time he had to head back for the rest of his shift, there would be a lot more people strolling around.

But until that time, he allowed himself to enjoy the peace. The quiet had been something Alex had found incredibly strange when he'd first moved to Greenford. All he'd ever known was the noise and chaos of living in Port Dale for his entire life and not having the sounds of loud cars, drunken arguments, the occasional gunshot, and all manner of other things that came with living in the city had been an adjustment.

Even the college campus was quiet at the busiest hours when compared to the streets he'd grown up on. Most conversations were kept to a dull roar as the students walked around, and when there was next to no one, all that could be heard was the wind and the rustling of the branches. He supposed there were probably plenty of noisy places on the campus, but he'd yet to come across any.

His steps stuttered to a stop when he reached the front of the administration building. There, on a small grass hill just in front of the building was Cid. Rather than patiently waiting somewhere near the path, however, the man was sprawled on his back, staring up at the sky with a content expression on his face.

Cid looked up as Alex approached, his quiet expression suddenly brightening. "Oh, hey!"

"Hey yourself," Alex said, peering down at him. "What are you doing?"

"Watching the sky?"

"You look ridiculous."

"I note from your tone that that's not really a criticism."

No, he supposed it wasn't. The words had left his mouth before he could think about them. And yeah, seeing a full-grown man in slacks and a dress shirt sprawled out on the side of a hill was a little ridiculous looking. But it was really hard to argue with the sight when Cid was so clearly happy about what he was doing.

"I like the sun," Cid explained, pushing himself to his feet and gently brushing his slacks clean of stray blades of grass. "When it gets warm and sunny out, and you know winter is finally behind us and we get to enjoy nice days like this."

"Always meant that it was about to get hotter than hell to me," Alex said with a shrug.

"Oh yeah, you never did tell me where you were from," Cid pointed out.

"Port Dale," Alex said, figuring it was a safe enough piece of information to hand out.

Cid hummed thoughtfully as they began to walk. "I've never been down that way. I hear it's a nice enough place to visit."

"It can be, I guess, if you're just visiting and staying out of the neighborhood I grew up in," Alex admitted.

"That's probably true of a lot of cities," Cid said with a chuckle. "I guess everywhere is bound to have its not-so-great places. And I generally stay away from them. I'd probably last a minute."

"That's not a bad thing," Alex told him as they walked across the stretch of grass that led to the nearby street. "People who can live in that kind of place aren't exactly the happiest people."

"So, you weren't happy?" Cid asked.

Alex shrugged. "I think I was just...surviving. That's pretty much all you could do when you were stuck there. Eh, some people didn't survive, though. Some just...got stuck in a rut and ended up getting hooked on something, getting killed, going to jail, whatever."

"Or like you, they get out?" Cid asked.

"Yeah, I guess some of them do," Alex said softly, thinking of Rio.

The agreement with the Los Muertos had been that so long as Alex did some jobs here and there, they would leave Rio out of their business. At some point, they'd decided that having just one brother working for them wasn't enough. They wanted the set. Alex hadn't known that they'd pulled Rio into a couple of deals when he wasn't around, slowly trying to get him to work with them as well. Rio was a good-looking guy with a bright personality, he would have been a perfect representative for the Los Muertos when they were trying to rope in new people.

Yet, not only had they broken their agreement with Alex, but they hadn't followed through on keeping Rio safe. They'd got a little too eager to put Rio's personality to the test and sent him out with a couple of people. Alex still didn't know why Rio had done it in the first place, maybe he too wanted to help keep the household afloat, or maybe there was another reason. All he knew was that when someone from a nearby rival gang had decided to shoot a few rounds into the group, it had been Rio who'd taken the bullets while the two Los Muertos members had dived for cover.

The local man in charge had told Alex all this, shrugging when he reached the end and told Alex, "That's how business goes sometimes." Alex had thought about that a lot when he'd left the dirty office located in one of the many warehouses that littered the edge of Port Dale. And he'd thought about it even more when he'd made a call, one that would inevitably have him removed from the city and placed under federal protection.

"I hit a nerve, didn't I?" Cid asked softly.

Alex looked up, realizing that they'd walked almost a block in complete silence. "I...it's not your fault. I don't want to talk too much about it but, last year, my little brother was killed. It's not exactly a happy memory, and it's why I left Port Dale and ended up here."

The somber, sorrowful expression on Cid's face looked so out of place when Alex was used to seeing him smile and laugh. "I'm sorry, Alex, I didn't mean to drag that back up for you."

"You didn't," Alex said, shaking his head. "Comes up on its own. It doesn't need anyone else's help."

Which was completely true. Alex could go about his days completely fine and then out of nowhere, the grief would roll through him in a steady wave of blue and black. Something as simple as seeing an advertisement for that goofy ghost hunting show Rio had loved so much could draw upon what felt like an infinite well of sorrow. There were days where he sometimes forgot Rio was gone and expected to find him nearby or waiting back in the apartment.

So no, his grief didn't need any help. It was strong enough on its own.

"If it's that hard, I don't want you to talk about it," Cid told him, stopping outside a cafe.

"I should talk about him," Alex said, watching the people across the street as they walked along the sidewalk, chatting merrily to one another. "Not about what happened to him, but him. He deserves that much."

"What was his name?"

"Rio."

"What about the rest of your family?"

"Dad took off forever ago, and my mom's always been

more interested in her next fix than anything else. I doubt she's even noticed either of us is gone. Shit, she could be dead for all I know, it's bound to happen eventually."

Though he suspected that was less to do with any danger from the Los Muertos than it was from her own drug habit. It was no small secret that there was no love between Alex and his mother. She was the reason he had to hide the money he did make. Otherwise, she would have stolen it and used it for her next hit instead of the bills or groceries as Alex would have. There had been far too many arguments in that old apartment over the money Alex 'kept' from her.

So, he highly doubted they would even bother to talk to her to find out where he was. Alex hadn't told his mother anything, not that she would have cared save to want him gone as quickly as possible. Turning on the Los Muertos was a death sentence for anyone who was caught, so she would have been more than happy to see the back of him. And if they did happen to come for her, well, Alex couldn't quite summon the ability to care about that either.

"I'm really bad at this conversation thing, aren't I?" Cid asked with a wince.

Alex had to laugh at that. "No, it's not your fault I come with a bunch of fucked up shit in my life. Hell, all this should be making you run in the other direction."

"Mmm," Cid hummed thoughtfully, screwing up his face. "Nah, don't wanna."

"It's what any smart person would do."

"Then I guess I'm not very smart, but that's okay."

Alex shook his head, unable to keep the wonder off his face. "How do you manage that?"

"Manage what?" Cid asked curiously.

Alex motioned to him. "Just...I know you've had to go

through some shit before. Even if you didn't have a shitty time in the system, it still couldn't have been great."

"Eh, sometimes it was pretty good," Cid said with a shrug. "Sometimes it wasn't."

Alex couldn't imagine being shipped all over the place like that, never having a place to call home. Even though the shitty apartment he'd grown up in wasn't exactly full of great memories, but it had at least been something, somewhere to call home. Cid hadn't had that for most of his life, being shunted around lives and families as he grew up. Alex couldn't imagine anyone would come out of that sort of arrangement well adjusted.

"I just," Alex began, still trying to wrap his head around it. "You're so happy, and you take things like...I mean, someone can give you shit and you just shrug it off. The only time I've seen you not happy is when you hear what people might say about me or when you thought you got me all sad."

Cid laughed at that. "Well, I think that's fair, don't you? In case you haven't noticed, I do kind of like you already, and I don't want people to talk badly about you. And I don't want to make people sad either, especially when I care about them. Why shouldn't any of that make sense?"

Alex sighed, shaking his head. He had no idea how someone so bright, cheerful, and full of life would be interested in him, but it was hard to turn it away when Cid was staring at him with earnest appreciation on his face.

Before he could second guess himself, he reached out and took hold of the man's face, pulling him close. Cid gave a soft sound of surprise but came willingly as Alex pressed their lips together, kissing him. He was a little surprised to find Cid pressed tighter into the kiss, his body coiling up tightly as he grabbed tight to Alex's shirt. There had been absolutely no hesitation in Cid's response, and it was as passionate as it had been immediate.

"Wow," Cid muttered as Alex slowly drew back. "Wasn't expecting that."

Neither had Alex, but he wasn't going to complain either. His body felt like it was buzzing, and it was becoming increasingly difficult not to try to find a way to pull the man somewhere more quiet and secluded. As it was, everyone on the street and in the nearby cafe would have been witness to everything.

"I see happy and cheerful doesn't mean well-behaved," Alex observed, torn between wanting to kiss the man again and waiting for a far more private moment to revisit it.

Cid's eyes sparkled as he grinned. "Oh, trust me, they're not at all mutually exclusive."

Which made his already tightening pants feel even more constraining than they had before. Alex was incredibly glad that his jacket hung down over the crotch of his pants. Otherwise, he would run the risk of putting on a show for anyone who took a look.

He was definitely going to have to kiss the man again, and he was most certainly going to have to put Cid's almost challenge to the test as well. But while they stood in full view of way too many people, he was going to behave himself.

Cid smiled knowingly at him. "Let's go get some lunch. And maybe some caffeine while we're at it. This place has amazing espresso."

"Oh God," Alex groaned as Cid opened the door to let them in. "I can only imagine you with caffeine in your system."

Cid's laughter trailed behind him as Alex followed him in. And it was only then he realized that had been the first time he'd ever kissed another man in a public space. That it had been with Cid somehow made perfect sense, and Alex barely spared a glance around the small cafe as they entered. Instead, he kept his eyes on the way Cid's eyes lit up as he looked over the menu and the small dimples on the sides of his mouth as he beamed at the barista.

CID

With Friday night upon him, Cid busied himself getting the house ready. Not that there was a whole lot to clean up, he had recently gone through a spate of cleaning that had lasted for a couple of hours. He also didn't want the house to be spotless. Cid had always found it strange to visit someone's home and see it completely free of any mess or rather signs of habitation.

"Doing alright in there, Gus?" he asked the ball python.

As expected, the snake did little but flick its tongue out, sensing that he was near. It was currently curled up on its heating rock, content and happy after having been fed a couple of hours before. Cid made sure the water in the bowl was fresh before leaving the snake to its borderline comatose state.

He honestly had no idea what sort of things Alex might like to watch or if the offer to watch movies together had just been a front for something far more sexual. Then again, he supposed that was the beauty of streaming services, all the variety, none of the commitment. And because he wasn't exactly what one would call a fantastic cook, he'd decided to wait until Alex showed up and the two of them could decide on a pizza to enjoy together.

He looked around, making sure he hadn't left something lying out. He was terrible about drinking coffee and leaving the mugs lying around. And it was never in the most obvious places, like the metal and glass coffee table by his living room or the small dining room table he had shoved into the corner because the room was tiny. No, it had to be on the top of a bookshelf that contained his random assortment of books and movies, on the shelf at the top of the hallway closet, and one time he'd found one still half-full and ice cold on the small shelves in his bathtub.

Cid perked up when he heard the sound of a car door outside. Going to the front window, he pulled the drapes aside to see Alex stepping out of the backseat of a car. He'd obviously got a ride through an app, but Cid could have sworn the man had a car of his own.

He met Alex at the front door, cocking his head. "Car trouble?"

Alex huffed. "Fucking brake line went out. I'm frigging lucky all I hit was a light post in a parking lot. Probably would have wrapped my car around one of the thousands of trees around town."

"Damn," Cid said, looking him over worriedly. "How did that happen?"

Alex shrugged, scowling. "Car was a piece of shit, but I guess it was a bigger piece of shit than I thought. Stupid line was worn down. It was apparently a miracle it didn't go out on me sooner. So now I'm gonna have to figure out if I want to fork over for repairs or just get a new...are you examining me right now?"

Cid froze, realizing he had been caught out scrutinizing

Alex's limbs for any bruising and watching him for any signs of pain. "If I said no, would you believe me?"

"No."

"Ah, well, then yeah, I guess I was."

"It was a lamppost, Cid, and I was going like, maybe five. My day was more bruised than my car."

"Injuries can happen at any time," Cid told him, albeit a little sheepishly.

"If I can take being stabbed, I think I can manage my car bumping into a light post," Alex told him with a huff. "Now, can I come in or are we going to hang out on your front step the whole time?"

"Oh," Cid said, a little thrown off by Alex's revelation. "Right, yeah, come in."

He supposed he shouldn't have been too surprised to find out Alex had apparently been stabbed in the past. The man hadn't exactly tried to hide the fact that he'd come from a rough neighborhood and dealt with some tough things. Still, it was something else entirely to find out the man had actually been assaulted with a potentially lethal weapon.

"Cozy," Alex said, kicking off his shoes after closing the door behind him.

Cid snorted. "I'm renting it. I was just coming here to do my residency, so I didn't want to buy anything. But after being here for a little while, I don't know, I think I might actually want to stick around for a while."

Alex nodded. "Can see why. It was kinda weird at first, coming from Port Dale and living here, but I'm getting used to it. Nice to be able to sleep with the windows open and all you're gonna hear is bugs and wind, instead of the neighbors screaming at each other in another drunken fight."

"I had neighbors like that when I was going through

med school," Cid told him with a wrinkle of his nose. "I always wondered what they saw in each other, but uh, after I was still around for the end of the fight, I figured it out."

Alex snorted. "Let me guess, their makeup sex was great."

"Apparently it was phenomenal for them both," Cid said with a shake of his head. "Don't know about you, but doesn't matter how good the sex is, I don't think it's worth fighting with someone all the time."

"Yeah, cut out the drama bullshit and just let it be great sex with someone, and I'm good."

Cid grinned wickedly at that. "Can't argue with that kind of logic."

Alex's returning smirk sent a flash of heat through Cid as they stood before his front door, watching each other. Considering Alex had already taken the initiative, Cid stepped into the man's space and pressed their lips together. He was delighted to find Alex's hand wrapped itself around his waist and pulled him in closer, parting their lips as he kissed him back fervently.

"Talk about good sex and then kiss me," Alex pointed out. "Subtle."

"Purely a coincidence," Cid assured him, though he knew his grin was giving him away.

"Sure," Alex said, his hand slipping to cup Cid's ass and squeeze. "Keep telling yourself that."

Yeah, Cid was beginning to think it had been a good idea to grab a new pack of condoms to throw in the bedroom earlier that day. While he hadn't wanted to say for sure that anything was going to happen, his suspicions had been there. It wasn't like either of them had been all that shy about mentioning sex or being flirtatious with each other. And the fact that it came with them spending time together and getting to know one another in the meantime was, Cid thought, a great sign.

"Mm, you hungry?" Cid asked, feeling his stomach grumble softly.

"Might be," Alex said with another squeeze.

Cid laughed. "I meant for actual food. Apparently, kissing you is a really bad idea if I want to have a serious conversation."

"Maybe it is."

Once more, Cid felt a wash of heat go through him, curling in his gut at the sound of the other man's voice. Alex naturally had a deep rumble to his voice as it was, but when he wanted to, he could make it go impossibly deep and with just the right amount of a growl to it. Cid had absolutely no trouble imagining how that would sound when it was right in his ear while Alex slid himself inside.

Cid cleared his throat. "Well, I can't cook...very well. So, I figured we could just get a pizza and call it good."

Alex watched him and Cid was struck by the sudden feeling of being hunted. "Sounds good. Just no pineapple or olives. I'm not coming anywhere near you if you put that shit on a perfectly good pizza."

Cid snorted, reluctantly stepping away from Alex. "Duly noted. Let me grab my phone and I can make the order. You go make yourself comfortable."

Leaving Alex where he stood, Cid stepped into the nearby dining room, looking around for his phone. One of the many reasons he was constantly suffering from damaged phones was his tendency to leave the devices lying just about anywhere. And like his tendency with coffee mugs, he could leave his phones in the strangest of places at times.

"Oh shit," he heard Alex say from the other room with a laugh. "You've got a fucking snake."

Cid spotted his phone on one of the dining room chairs, snatching it up as he called back. "Yeah, that's Gus."

Alex waited until Cid came into the living room to speak again. "Never woulda pegged you as someone to have a snake. You seem like a dog person."

"I like dogs," Cid admitted as he opened up the app. "And cats. Rabbits. Hamsters are a little evil, but I like them. And I like lizards and snakes. Gus was an old roommate's snake, but after he dropped out he had to go back to his parent's and there was no way his mom was going to let him bring a snake into her house. So I offered to take her."

"Wait," Alex looked up from the terrarium. "Gus is a she?"

Cid laughed. "My roommate didn't know it was a female when he named her. Kind of figured it out after we'd been calling her Gus for ages, so it just kind of stuck."

Alex shook his head. "You really have weirdness in every part of your life, in the smallest ways, don't you?"

Cid hadn't really thought about it like that, but he had to admit there was some truth to that statement. "I like to think of it as charm, just charm everywhere, charm, charm, and charm."

"Uh-huh," Alex said, watching Gus. "What's she doing?"

"Food coma."

"You fed her?"

"A few hours ago, so she's gonna be pretty content for a while."

"What, you just...throw a mouse in there and call it good?"

Cid shook his head. "Nah, that's a bad idea. You could risk the snake getting injured if the mouse is big enough and willing to fight back or something. Gotta give them some frozen mice you warm up. Which uh, side note, if you go looking for ice or something later, don't grab one of the frozen mice instead."

Alex snorted. "Thanks, I'll try not to drop a dead mammal in my drink."

"Food's ordered," Cid told him, sliding the phone away. "Should be here in another hour. Want to get the movies started?"

"Sure," Alex shrugged, turning to look at the entertainment system behind him. "Jesus. How much do you spend on electronics?"

"Um, a lot? I don't know. It's mostly for gaming, but I get some movies in once in a while. You can pick the first one, though," Cid told him. "I'm going to go grab a couple of beers for us from the fridge."

"Ooh, pizza, beer, and the hint of seeing you naked later?" Alex asked with a grin. "How the fuck has no one snatched you up and kept you by now?"

Cid hesitated at the doorway. "I guess no one wanted to."

"Fuckin' weird," Alex muttered as he fiddled with the TV to get it going.

Cid only smiled as he stepped out of the room to go get the beers. Maybe that was a sign Alex might be interested in a long time instead of just a good one.

A FEW HOURS and a handful of beers apiece later, and Cid was feeling pretty good. He knew part of it was definitely the alcohol, but really, it was just nice to have someone around. Especially when that someone was Alex, who had all but sprawled across Cid's couch and left Cid with very little room to sit and so was forced to lean against him, between the man's legs.

"Damn," Alex muttered, taking another sip of his beer as they watched the latest movie. "So he was dead the whole time? That's fucked up."

Cid laughed, comfortable with his head pressed against the lower part of Alex's thick thigh. "There's little signs of it throughout the movie. Like, if you go back and watch it again, you'll see that he's been wearing the same shirt the whole time."

"No shit?" Alex asked. "That's pretty sneaky."

Cid grinned but kept quiet as the movie worked its way to the final few minutes. He'd been a little surprised to find out Alex hadn't really seen a lot of movies that would be considered must-see. So after sorting through the ones available, Cid had finally settled on one he thought might impress.

And he was seriously going to have to make the man watch the Terminator movies at some point.

"Huh," Alex said once the credits started rolling. "Don't like creepy shit, but that was pretty good."

"Told you," Cid said proudly.

Alex looked down at him. "Someone's feeling smug."

"Just a little," Cid said, distracted as he felt the muscles of Alex's legs flex beneath him.

"So how long you been between my legs?" Alex asked with a smirk.

"Like you haven't been paying attention the whole time," Cid said with a roll of his eyes.

He knew full well the man had noticed, if only because Cid had been blatantly trying to avoid noticing the man's physical reaction to their proximity. That had been easier said than done, especially when Cid had also spotted just why it would have been difficult for Alex to keep his arousal concealed. There really didn't seem to be anything about the man that was small.

"I might've, but then someone went and put an interesting movie on," Alex said, draining the last bit of his beer.

A thrill rippled through Cid, and he let his hand slide a little further up Alex's thigh. "Does that mean you're paying attention again?"

Alex rolled from being partially on his side to on his back, staring at Cid intently. "Trust me, if you had started doin' something that woulda got my attention, I wouldn't have given a fuck about the movie."

"Well, that's good to know," Cid said, giving Alex's thigh a squeeze. The effect was immediate and he could see the front of Alex's jeans bulging outward as he once more got the man's attention.

"Just be sure you know what you're starting," Alex warned him, though there was still a smirk on his face.

"Ah, I'm not all that worried," Cid told him, getting up to kneel between Alex's legs and lean over him. He cupped the man's groin, sucking in his bottom lip as he felt the man's cock grow even harder and thicker under his touch. "Big men don't scare me."

Alex's dark eyes grew even darker as Cid leaned in. "I can get a little rough sometimes too."

Cid grinned at that. "That a promise?"

He didn't give Alex the chance to respond, however, closing the distance between them and kissing the man. He felt Alex buck up into his touch, grinding against Cid's palm as their lips parted. Cid managed to undo the man's pants just as their tongues slid over one another, dipping his fingers beneath the waistband of Alex's pants and gripping the base of his cock. Alex groaned softly as Cid rotated his hand, carefully extracting Alex's cock from the confines of his jeans.

Cid gave a low moan as he slid his grip over the entirety of the shaft, feeling out its girth and weight against his fingers. Alex was definitely big, but not so big as to be absolutely terrifying either. Cid had absolutely no doubt he would have no problem with whatever Alex had to throw at him, and in fact, looked forward to it.

He broke the kiss, releasing Alex's cock so he could shove the man's shirt upward. Cid was rewarded by an expanse of skin and muscle, with the man's chest and shoulders covered in ink. Whoever had taken their needle to Alex was no hack. A colorful bird, either a peacock or a phoenix, curled its way around one pec, its long tail sweeping over his shoulder. Snakes, or possibly stylized dragons, wrapped around the other shoulder, disappearing into the sleeve. A paragraph of text that Cid couldn't read was etched onto the man's ribs.

But Alex's stomach was completely free of any ink, leaving the bare skin covered in a fine layer of dark hair on full display. Cid's eyes ran over the long lines on the man's stomach and lingered on the puckered marks on his left side. Apparently, when Alex had mentioned getting stabbed, he had decided to leave out that it hadn't just been one jab.

Running his hand over Alex's chest and down his stomach, he felt his own gut tighten. The man was no stranger to physical labor, and from the little scars his fingertips picked up that his eyes couldn't in the dimly lit living room, he was no stranger to a hard life as well.

That certainly didn't have any effect on Alex's ability to groan low and pleasantly when Cid finally bent down and took him into his mouth. Cid was delighted to find that the man was already leaking from his excitement, the tasty and welcome addition to the weight of the man's cock on his tongue. Even better, Alex was not shy about groaning even louder when Cid managed to take almost all of him into his throat with one swift push forward.

Alex's fingers curled in his hair, pulling him firmly down onto his cock. The last couple of inches didn't go as smoothly as the first handful had, but Cid worked his throat, drawing a growl from the man. He was already loving how vocal the other man was and drew back only to push himself down again, taking Alex almost to the hilt.

"Fucking hell," Alex hissed, his grip tightening in Cid's hair. "Where the fuck did you learn to do that?"

Cid only responded by doing it again, groaning when he had Alex almost completely in. The effect had Alex's hips jerking up toward him as the man gave another low noise of pleasure. Cid didn't hesitate to repeat it, occasionally letting Alex take over so the man could thrust up into his throat. Cid also had to admit, between the messy sounds he was making as he repeatedly took Alex's thick cock into his throat and the low, almost growls Alex was making, he was thoroughly enjoying himself.

Alex's grip on him grew stronger and he pulled Cid up and off his cock with a low growl. Before Cid could say anything, he found himself pulled upward as though he weighed nothing, and his lips crashed against Alex's. The kiss was hard, Alex's stubble scraping against Cid's cheeks as he held tight to his face.

"I guess I should dig out those condoms and lube," Cid said, trying to laugh but barely managing the sound.

"Be quick," Alex told him.

Cid was more than happy to do that, though he was less happy about having to separate himself from Alex. The bedroom was just down the hall and he darted in, pulling off his shirt as he went. Tossing it on the floor, he undid his pants and yanked open the drawer next to the bed. Cid had shown a little bit of foresight when he'd bought the condoms, suspecting but not absolutely sure which ones he would need. As he shoved his pants off with one hand, he grabbed the box of large condoms and the bottle of lube as well, kicking his pants aside.

At least he'd been prepared.

ALEX

He couldn't help but snort as he heard Cid thumping around somewhere. The guy had all but leaped off the couch, flying through the house to get what they needed. Admittedly, Alex could relate. His own heart was thumping furiously as he waited eagerly for the other man to reappear.

While he waited, he shoved off his pants and underwear, kicking them onto the floor. His shirt came next before he finally flopped back onto the couch, feeling far more comfortable. Curling his fingers around his cock, he gave a few lazy strokes, more than happy to think about the blowjob he'd been receiving and had to interrupt.

Honestly, if he hadn't stopped Cid, the man would have got Alex off in record time. Alex might have been embarrassed about that, but he thought it would have said more about Cid's skill than any failing on his part. He never would have imagined that someone so perky and seemingly innocent could suck dick with such skill and enthusiasm, but he was more than happy to be wrong.

The thumping drew closer and Alex picked his head up as Cid came hurrying into the room. Somewhere along the way, he had lost his clothes, which were probably thrown haphazardly deeper in the house.

"Nice," Alex said, looking over Cid's body.

He'd know the man was probably in good shape. Cid didn't exactly dress to show off his body, but he didn't try to hide it either. Under the dress shirts and slacks that he'd seen Cid wear, Alex had noticed the signs of a body that was used to being taken care of. Seeing it revealed, however, was a completely different experience.

Cid wasn't nearly as pale as Alex thought he might be, so the man either saw a decent amount of sunlight or was no stranger to a tanning bed. Although he was only a little shorter than Alex, his shoulders were slightly narrower, and his frame was more trim. Cid wasn't what Alex would have called bulky, but he could definitely imagine the man in a speedo and goggles, looking comfortable in a pool.

Cid looked down, where he was sporting only a pair of thin and tiny trunks. "What?"

"Get your ass over here so I can pull those things off you," Alex growled. Even with the distance and the dim lighting, he could see Cid's cock threatening to tear through the fabric.

The other man did as was told, with the same enthusiasm and grin on his face like he seemed to do just about everything else. Alex leaned up, grabbing hold of him and dragging Cid down onto the couch with him. Cid came willingly, though with a laugh as he was pinned against the couch.

Alex did exactly as he promised, grabbing the man's underwear and yanking them down to Cid's knees so they could be easily removed. Cid wriggled for a moment to get them off and then stilled when Alex's hand wrapped around his cock.

He smirked. "Give me what you got, and get those legs in the air."

"Bossy," Cid said, still grinning as he handed the packet and bottle over.

Alex took them as Cid obeyed the rest of the command. He let the foil wrapper drop before opening up the bottle and spreading lube over his fingers. It was the only warning Cid got before Alex slid two fingers inside him, sucking in a sharp breath as he felt the warm grip close around his fingers.

Cid's back arched as Alex worked his fingers inside him. Among the soft noises Cid was making, Alex bent down between his legs, kissing the man fiercely just as he added a third. The grip around his fingers was tight, but it wasn't ferocious. Apparently, Cid was more than aware of how to make himself relax.

The other man moaned into the kiss as Alex spread his fingers apart before finally adding a fourth one. It seemed like the more he gave Cid, the more the man was able to take. Which not only added a few extra beats a minute to his own heart rate but meant Cid hadn't been kidding about not being worried.

Alex snatched up the foil packet from the couch cushion, opened it and with a little lube from his hand, rolled the condom on. As fond as he was of a lot of different positions, there was no way in hell he was going to pass up the chance to see Cid's face while he fucked him into the couch.

When the head of his cock pushed into Cid, their sounds were in unison. Even through the layer of the condom, Alex could feel the tight heat of the other man wrapping around the thick head of his cock as he sank in another inch.

Cid tried to wrap his legs around Alex, but with a sharp

shake of his head, Alex pushed them back up so they rested on his shoulders. His eyes darted between where his cock slowly sank into the other man and then up to Cid's face. Even in the dim light coming from the TV, Cid's bright eyes glimmered, marked by the swollen pupils.

Alex was a little amazed at how quickly he was able to push inside Cid. Prepared and skilled at relaxing himself wouldn't have been enough to completely negate the pressure and possible ache of being entered by someone of Alex's size. Yet Cid had barely winced as Alex had pushed in deep, finally embedding himself completely in the other man.

It was probably the fastest he'd ever been able to get inside of someone else. He shivered as the last inch slid into Cid, drawing a low moan from the other man as he clung to Alex's wrists.

"Fuck, how do you do that?" Alex asked, delaying for a moment to bring himself under control.

"What?" Cid asked, breathing heavily.

"Take that so easily."

"Easily? No, that stung."

"Then why didn't you say something?"

Cid laughed at that, reaching up to run a hand down Alex's stomach. "Because this is hot. A little bit of 'ow' when like...it's this hot, but it's pretty okay with me. I told you I can take it."

Somehow he shouldn't have been surprised that, as resilient as Cid was, the man could probably take a good pounding as well. Then again, he was more than a little impressed and just because he'd personally taken Alex so well. Alex had bottomed before, and he had to say the experience left him more than a little respectful of guys who could do it so readily.

"Guess that's my cue," Alex grumbled, easing his hips back to slide his cock almost free of Cid.

As he pushed back in, he didn't know what had caused the pang of lust to jolt through him. The sight of him sliding deep into the man's body was pure eroticism, but the way Cid's mouth fell open, moaning desperately, was almost enough to send him over the edge. If things kept going the way they were, he wasn't so sure he was going to be able to maintain his stamina. Watching Cid react to Alex's cock sliding deep inside him was an experience all its own, and Alex was suddenly sure he wanted to see that expression on the man's face quite often, though maybe not as much as the goofy smile the man was so fond of giving.

Emboldened not only by their brief conversation but Cid's reaction, Alex decided to test the theory. On the next stroke, he snapped his hips forward, managing to almost entirely bury himself in Cid with one movement. Cid's back arched up into it, his fingers digging into Alex's thighs as he gave a cry of pleasure.

And that was all Alex needed.

His pace picked up after that, slamming himself down into the other man. When the thrusts were hard enough that Cid's body threatened to bounce off the couch, Alex moved his grip. Sliding his hand up, he wrapped his fingers around the base of Cid's neck, pressing his palm against the man's collarbone to hold him in place. To his mild surprise, Cid stretched his neck, pushing his ass up into Alex's thrusts with renewed vigor.

Alex wouldn't have quite called it brutal, as it lacked the pure lust and drive for release that had come with the few times he'd had considerably rough sex. But there was a fire between them as Alex drove himself into Cid, no longer caring if he was going to last or not. All he knew was that every time he buried himself deep, Cid would cry out or groan.

And then, Cid's body went wire tight beneath him, holding tight enough onto Alex's arm and thigh that Alex felt a sharp stab of pain. His body bore down around Alex's cock, gripping it fiercely as Cid cried out, his cock jerking between them as he covered his own stomach and chest.

Without missing a beat, Alex pulled himself free from inside Cid. With a flick of his wrist, he yanked the condom off and tossed it onto the floor without a look. It took only a few strokes of his cock and he cried out, hunching over Cid as he came, adding his own layer to the mess that was pooling on Cid's neck.

Panting for breath, Alex dropped back onto his haunches, chest heaving for air. Cid went completely boneless, legs splaying against the back of the couch and onto the floor. His cheeks were flushed, eyes still darkened by the wide pupils, and a wide, extremely satisfied smile on his face.

"Cum covered looks good on you," Alex said, looking him over.

"How about well-fucked? Because I'm feeling pretty well-fucked at the moment," Cid said with a low, throaty chuckle.

"Oh, you definitely look that, also a good look for you. Really, you looked good with my dick inside you too."

Cid closed his eyes, humming softly. "We've got to get a picture or video of that because I know I'd want to see it. Maybe a mirror?"

Alex narrowed his eyes, the corner of his mouth twitching. "You really are a lot dirtier than I gave you credit for? What's next, fucking in public?"

Cid opened one eye. "Only if it's somewhere we probably won't get busted."

Alex laughed, bending down to kiss the man gently. "Fine."

He held off from saying that he didn't want anyone else getting a look at Cid's ass, but just barely. They weren't exactly a couple, or at least, Alex didn't think they'd somehow slipped into that territory without realizing it. Yet the urge to make some sort of claim, other than covering the man in his cum, had risen strongly in him for a brief moment.

"Let's get you cleaned up before you start getting sticky," Alex muttered against his lips.

Both of Cid's eyes opened, and they were bright blue and sparkling happily. "Stay the night?"

"Yeah," Alex said before he even thought about what he was agreeing to. "I can do that."

CID HAD INEVITABLY GIVEN up on trying to use a towel to clean himself and had chosen to hop in the shower to rinse off. While he'd done that, Alex had cleaned up their mess in the living room, munching on some leftover pizza as he went. It only took Cid a few minutes to emerge, as naked as he went in and still a little wet from the shower.

"Damn," Cid said when he caught sight of Alex.

Alex froze, the last bite of a slice of pizza at his lips. "What?"

"You'd think after what just happened, I'd be a little calmer. But just seeing you walk around, your cock hanging out, with that body and just...you?" Cid said, leaning against the doorway and staring at Alex. "Yeah, no, I guess I'm not that calm at all."

"That so?" Alex asked with a raised brow.

Cid grinned. "Believe it or not, but you're big enough that I can still feel you in me right now. And that's probably not helping."

Alex's stomach twisted pleasantly. "Christ, you've got a fuckin' mouth on you, don't you?"

The boy next door looks did not betray the filthy mind that apparently Cid possessed.

Cid grinned. "Sadly, the spirit is willing, but the body needs at least a few hours to recover from the pounding it just took."

Which did little to turn away the now buzzing warmth and interest that was settling back into Alex's mind. How the hell he had managed to find someone as bright and warm as Cid, who apparently liked Alex for whatever reason and was able to keep up with him if not actually outpace him, he didn't know. What he did know was that it was becoming harder and harder to tell himself that whatever was going on between them couldn't or shouldn't probably last.

Cid narrowed his eyes. "Hmm, can't tell if the thought I just saw cross your face was a good one or a bad one."

Alex popped the piece of pizza into his mouth, chewed and swallowed before shaking his head. "I'll let you know when I figure it out."

Cid smiled at that. "Fair enough."

And then Cid was stepping closer to him, wrapping his arms around Alex's waist and drawing him in for a kiss. It was nothing like the other kisses, which had been either sudden or with desire pulsing heavily behind them. Instead, it was slow and sweet, and Alex felt his attention gliding over Cid's naked body pressed against him and the sensation of his lips against his as he hummed happily.

"It's kind of late," Cid said. "Ready to go lay down?"

"Yeah," Alex said, heart feeling as though it were tripping over itself. "I think that would be a good idea."

Cid gave him a smile, one a little more tired-looking than the others but sweet all the same. Taking Alex's hand in his, Cid led the way back toward the bedroom, turning off the lights as they went. The bed was more than big enough for the both of them, but as soon as Alex got beneath the covers, Cid rolled over and pressed himself against Alex's chest.

"This okay?" Cid asked as though sensing Alex's surprise.

Alex snorted, wrapping an arm around Cid's back and holding him there. "I'm just not used to it, is all."

"Used to what?"

"I mean, after I fuck someone, they're generally good to go."

"They leave?"

"Or I do. Cuddling ain't exactly something that people really wanted out of me."

"That's a shame. Because based on what I'm getting right now, you're definitely a good cuddler."

That, even more than Cid's blatant appreciation of Alex's body and bedroom skills, warmed Alex in a way that left him speechless. It was beginning to feel like every time he thought he might find his footing, Cid would find some way, in his sweet and earnest manner, to knock Alex on his ass once more. He honestly wished circumstances were different, maybe then he wouldn't feel the nagging guilt at the back of his head.

Would he, though? He had to think about that question. Alex was sure he would have never met anyone like Cid if he'd still been living in Port Dale. His neighborhood didn't allow for people like Cid, not easily. His brother had been a lot like Cid in his cheerful demeanor, and the streets had been his undoing.

"There are things," Alex said suddenly as he lay in the dark, this wonderful man curled against him. "That I can't tell you."

"Can't, or won't?" Cid asked.

Alex sighed. It was a fair question. "Bit of both, but I'd probably be in deep shit if I did tell you."

"Like, in danger?"

Alex hesitated and then shook his head. "No. But there's going to be times where...I have to avoid a question you ask."

Cid pulled his head free from Alex's chest to look him in the face. "So, you want me to know that."

"Yeah," Alex said slowly, a little confused.

"Because you don't want to have to lie to me. You'd prefer to just tell me you can't talk about something in the future instead."

"Pretty much, yeah."

Cid smiled at him, leaning in to kiss him. "And that's a very good example of why I don't care that I know you've been purposefully keeping things from me. You're a good man, Alex, and I love that you're being so forthright with me. And if I ever dig too deep or pry too far, you just need to tell me and I'll back off."

"You'd do that, just like that?" Alex asked.

Cid shrugged. "Part of liking someone, of wanting to be with someone, is learning to trust them. And maybe I'm taking a risk by just...trusting that you've got a good reason for keeping things from me is my risk to take. So yeah, just like that."

"Be with, huh?" Alex asked softly.

Cid nodded, curling himself again so his face lay on Alex's chest. "If you want, when you want. I'm not like...trying to make you my boyfriend or anything like that. But I'd love the chance to find out if what's going on between us is going to stick and to find out what else there is to learn about one another."

"You are," Alex began in wonder, "one of the most absurdly accepting people I have ever met, do you know that?"

"I've had a lot of uncertainty in my life, Alex," Cid told him softly. "And my fair share of unhappiness. I *choose* to aim for happiness, and I also choose not to let the chaos and uncertainty of being alive get in the way of trying to be happy. So, this might be a mistake, or it could be even greater than I ever imagined it would be. But I want to choose it, and if you want to choose it too, then we can work together and find out where it's going to take us."

For someone who could come off as silly and overly playful, Cid was a lot more wise and practical than he appeared. There was something so ridiculously pragmatic about that viewpoint that even Alex couldn't find it in himself to argue with the other man.

Well, and he couldn't deny that the idea of turning his back on Cid, pretending they were never more than fuck buddies, brought an ugly twist to Alex's gut. There was no way he could ever treat Cid like that, and despite having only known the man briefly, he wanted to know even more and not stop knowing.

"I want to choose it too," Alex told him softly.

"Well," Cid said softly, a smile in his voice. "I guess we're going to find out where it leads us then."

CID

Day One

WAKING up on Saturday with Alex's presence in the bed had to rank up there as one of the best ways to wake up in Cid's mind. They had rolled apart at some point in the night, but that was just fine by Cid. He needed only to roll back over to press himself against Alex's back, wrapping his arms around the man's waist and squeezing.

"Mornin'," Alex grumbled, surprising Cid.

"I thought you were still sleeping," Cid mumbled against his neck.

Alex grunted. "Been kinda drifting back and forth over here for a bit."

Cid closed his eyes, nodding. "I never do that. When I'm awake, I'm awake."

But he was perfectly content to lay there, wrapped around the other man, listening to the sounds of his deep breathing. A smile graced his face as he remembered the night before. Cid had been wondering if Alex was willing to try for something a little more serious, and while they hadn't committed to one another, it was a good start.

"Kinda surprised you don't leap up out of bed the moment you wake up," Alex told him, nudging him.

Cid moved out of the way so Alex could roll onto his back. "Not going to lie to you, you're not completely wrong. I don't like to stay in bed, so when I know I'm awake, I just get started on my day. And since you're awake, I figure we could get some food in us and then figure out what we want to do with the rest of our day."

"Sounds good to me," Alex said as he eased onto his back, arms and legs splaying out as he stretched lazily.

Cid watched, enjoying the show as the man's body rippled with muscles shifting under his skin. Cid had no idea what the man's workout routine was, but he absolutely adored the results. It didn't hurt that the tattoos, and to an extent, the scars, just added to the raw strength that seemed to extend from Alex's body.

Though a quick glance toward Alex's groin told Cid that his strength wasn't the only thing extending.

He couldn't help but run his fingers over the muscles he could see moving on the man's chest and down his sides. That was until Alex tensed and jerked away from his touch.

"Quit," Alex grunted at him, swatting at his hands.

"Are you ticklish?" Cid asked in delight.

"I will kick you so hard if you try to tickle me," Alex warned with a glare.

Cid reached a hand out, hovering it over Alex's side. "That so?"

"Don't you touch me," Alex growled.

Which was a warning Cid had absolutely no intention of listening to. Though his attention shifted quickly from Alex's side, which the man was clearly prepared to guard, and more to his groin. Alex's hard-on had lessened, leaving it relatively soft but still impressive as it lay against his thigh. Which, of course, drew Cid's attention, and he quickly slipped his hand down to wrap his fingers around the shaft, stroking it gently.

Alex's guarded expression quickly became one of interest as he watched Cid's hand. The sleepy expression on his face was quickly overcome by the lustful expression Cid had been witness to the night before.

"That's not ticklish," Alex told him, his sleep roughened voice now rumbling pleasantly.

"Good thing I'm not trying to tickle you," Cid said, stomach tightening as he felt Alex's cock rapidly grow hard in his hand.

"You're a horndog," Alex told him even as his hands found their way to Cid's body to gently pull him closer.

Cid could only laugh at that because there was absolutely no denying it. The boyish looks everyone always attributed to him were not an indication of how innocent he was. Cid enjoyed sex, all manner of sex, and he wasn't going to be shy about it. And after the way Alex had taken over, not shy about using his strength to drill Cid into the couch and to an orgasm that had left him vaguely wondering if he'd forgotten his own name, he definitely wasn't going to be shy with Alex.

"Problem?" Cid asked innocently.

"Yeah, fuck that," Alex grunted, pushing Cid onto his back and sliding his own bulk over him.

"No, fuck me," Cid teased.

"That's the idea. Now I wanna see how flexible you really are."

Breakfast would have to wait.

DAY **Three**

"WELL, someone certainly looks proud of themselves," Dr. Finn commented as Cid breezed through the front door of the clinic.

"Uh, do I?" Cid asked, wondering how he was managing to look prideful.

"Well, more like the cat that got the canary. Good weekend?" Dr. Finn asked, her smile suddenly turning knowing.

"It was, thank you," Cid told her.

Cid would have absolutely not held it against Alex if the man hadn't decided to linger for the entire weekend. When Alex had gone in for half a shift, Cid had found himself wondering if the man would come back. Yet, a few hours later Alex returned, with his now repaired car as his means of transportation. They had spent the rest of their Sunday on the couch, watching more movies Alex apparently had missed out on while growing up.

"It was a very nice, relaxing weekend," Cid informed her as he clocked in through his work tablet.

"Right, and there's...nothing you want to tell me?" Dr. Finn asked, still grinning wide.

Cid chuckled. "You might as well just get it out of your system now."

"You totally had that guy over, didn't you?"

"I totally did."

"You spent the whole weekend with him."

"That I did."

"And you slept with him."

"Like bunnies."

Dr. Finn laughed, clapping her hands together in delight. "Aw, they grow up so fast."

Cid looked up, giving a startled laugh. "What? I'm almost thirty. I've been grown up."

"Not even here a year and you've already got yourself a boy toy. That's not so easy in a small town."

"First of all, it's a college town. Finding someone to sleep with isn't exactly difficult. Secondly, he's not a boy toy or anything like that," Cid corrected her, shaking his head.

"Oh, so it's serious?" Dr. Finn asked, cocking her head.

Cid shrugged, opening up the appointment list and combing over what was expected for the day. "We didn't sit down and proclaim our love for one another and dedicate ourselves to one another for life."

"You haven't known him for very long," Dr. Finn said with a snort. "I would be worried if you'd taken that big a step."

"We just decided there was something between us and we were going to figure out if it's going to last or not. So I guess we're...dating," Cid told her.

"Is that like, monogamously dating?"

Cid honestly didn't know. They hadn't exactly talked about whether they were going to exclusively be with one another. Still, honestly, Cid didn't know if it was something he should bring up or not.

"I mean, I don't have any intentions of seeing anyone else. But I mean, if he wants to see other people, I can't really stop him. That's his business," Cid told her, even as the thought caused an uncomfortable squirm in his gut.

Dr. Finn snorted. "He says, in a tone that says he'd rather pull his own teeth out instead."

Cid shrugged. "We didn't settle on that, didn't even talk

about it. To be honest, Alex isn't all that familiar with relationships and dating, and I'm rusty as hell."

Dr. Finn nodded. "So, you're taking things slow. That makes sense."

"I'm glad you think so. Now, am I allowed to get ready for the rest of my workday or do you want to know even more about my personal life?" Cid asked with a smirk.

"Yeah, is he hung?"

Cid walked away, shaking his head as he walked down the hallway to the sound of her laughter.

DAY **Six**

"SO JUST LIKE THAT, you guys decide to give it a try?" Alice asked, popping some of her chicken salad into her mouth.

Cid felt comfortable rolling his eyes, especially since they were closed and she wouldn't be able to see the gesture. The two of them had found a sunny spot in the grass outside of the Phys Ed building so they could chat and eat their lunch together. Of course, the conversation had been more about his budding relationship with Alex than anything else.

"Just like that," Cid repeated in a bored tone. "We'd seen enough of one another to decide we were okay with being a little more serious about seeing one another. Last I checked, that's how dating works."

"Well, I guess you didn't try to put a ring on it, so there's that," Alice said.

Cid cracked open an eye to peer up at her. "You're awfully doubtful for someone who doesn't even know him."

Alice shrugged unapologetically as she wiped at her mouth with a napkin. "Well, maybe I was being a little harsh about your first time seeing him. I'll own that. But for him to just straight up say he's not going to tell you shit? That's a little weird, don't you think?"

"Not really," Cid said. "People have good reasons for the things they do sometimes."

"Yeah, and sometimes, they only think they're good reasons when in reality, they're bullshit reasons," Alice told him.

"Cynic."

"Hopeless romantic."

Cid grinned. "I'll take that as something to be proud of."

"Good, then I'll do the same about being a cynic," Alice informed him.

"Whatever makes you feel better," Cid told her.

He knew his friend was only worried about him, and it was in her nature to be cautious, even to the point of paranoia. It didn't bother him, and in a way, he thought the two of them managed to balance each other out pretty well. And even if it didn't, neither of them were all that bothered by the other's attitude.

"So," Alice began slowly. "How's the sex?"

Cid sighed. "You really need to stop talking to Dr. Finn. You two are too much sometimes."

"Does that mean it's good or bad?"

"How did the topic turn to this?"

"Is he hung?"

"No, seriously. No more talking to Dr. Finn, this is getting creepy."

A familiar rumbling voice interrupted. "Oh. Hey."

Cid sat up quick enough that his shoulder slammed into Alice and almost knocked her over. Alex stood on the sidewalk leading toward the main lobby of the nearby building. His jeans were splattered with different colored stains, and his shirt was wet in a few spots. His dark eyes were locked on Cid, though occasionally darted toward Alice.

"Hey," Cid exclaimed after he made sure Alice was okay.

"Was coming to see if you wanted to catch lunch, but it looks like I'm too late," Alex explained, glancing at Alice again.

Alice, having finally stopped grumbling, snapped the lid on her salad. "And interrupted a great conversation. I was just finding out if you were any good in bed and if you were hung."

"Jesus," Cid groaned. "Alice!"

"Like a horse," Alex said without missing a beat. "And he's walked funny a couple of times, so I think I'm doing it right."

"Or doing him right," Alice corrected.

Alex shrugged, now smirking as he watched Alice. Cid, meanwhile, was torn between horror that the two of them were casually having the conversation and a little relieved at the same time because his best friend was chatting up Alex like it was nothing.

Alice glanced at Cid. "So, is he right?"

"Go away," Cid told her, refusing to make eye contact.

"He's such a prude," Alice said with a sigh, packing her things up.

"No," Alex said with a grin. "He's not."

"Oh ho," Alice said, returning the smile. "You and I are going to have to compare notes then. Because he never tells me anything good."

"No!" Cid barked out, jabbing a finger at Alex. "I can't stop her from asking, but don't you dare tell her anything. There are some things people don't need to know about me until it's important."

"See? No fun at all," Alice said, walking off with a wave. "You boys behave."

Alex waited until she was further away before approaching Cid and sitting next to him on the grass. "I guess that was Alice?"

Cid glared after her. "Yes, yes it was."

"She seems alright."

Cid threw up his hands. "Well, of course, she did to you. Apparently, neither of you have any shame."

"Weren't you the one who said we should find an empty classroom one of these days so I can bend you over the teacher's desk?"

"Yeah, so?"

"Right," Alex said with a snort. "So, just going to completely ignore the obvious connection there. That's fine."

Cid was going to do just that. And while he had Alex there with him, he was more than happy to lean over and lay his head on the man's shoulder. Finding a partner who was not just close to his height but actually taller than him was a rarity, and Cid loved the feeling of being smaller than the other man.

"You should have texted me," Cid told him. "Then I would have waited until you got your lunch and you could have joined us."

Alex shrugged, jostling Cid's head. "Someone stole my phone."

"What?"

"Yeah. I had it in the break room, thrown in a locker

because we were hosing down some of the outer walls today. And someone just...took it. No cameras there either, so I don't fucking know who did it."

"Geez," Cid said, taking Alex's hand in his. "I hope there was nothing important on it."

"Nah, not that I can think of. Old pictures, but I have those saved online, so it's not a big deal," Alex grunted, curling his fingers around Cid's.

"Not been having very good luck lately, have you?" Cid asked, thinking of the man's car.

Alex glanced at him, annoyance disappearing as he smiled. "I'd say my luck's been pretty good lately."

DAY **Nine**

"YOU SURE YOU'RE comfortable like that?" Alex asked him.

Cid peered up from where he sat on the floor in front of the couch. Alex sat behind him, his legs on each side of Cid. They were completely naked, with Cid's body still buzzing from their rowdy bout of sex about a half-hour before. A show on TV made good background noise, but Cid was content at the moment, sitting naked with the other man and soaking up the warmth of his body.

"Yeah," Cid told him, laying his head on the man's bare thigh once more.

"This your way of saying you like being between my legs?"

Cid laughed. "That's true, but not what I was going for."

Alex's hand slid into his hair, tugging gently. "Alright, I'm game. Explain it to me."

Cid smiled at that. Alex either had a lot of patience for Cid's habits or maybe, just maybe, the man actually liked hearing the random and usually long-winded thoughts that pinged around in Cid's skull.

"It's comfortable," Cid told him. "We're naked, had really great sex not that long ago, and I'm just relaxed. Sitting here, between your legs, nestled up against you, it's just like...comforting. It's warm, and it makes me feel safe, especially when you feel so relaxed and your fingers are in my hair. There's something...I don't know, soothing about it. Safe."

"So this is you feeling safe?" Alex asked.

"With you, yeah."

He couldn't see the other man's face, but he would swear he could hear the other man thinking. After a minute of silence, Alex's fingers resumed playing through his hair, tugging gently every now and then. The motion had been repeated several times over the past half hour, and it just added to the sensation of comfort and ease.

After about ten minutes, Alex spoke up again. "I'm glad I make you feel safe."

Cid smiled. "Good, because you do. There's just something comforting about you."

"Rio used to say that too," Alex mused. "When we'd hang out somewhere, probably somewhere we shouldn't have. Or just back in our shitty apartment. Told me it didn't matter where we were, he always felt safe when I was around."

It wasn't the first time Alex had mentioned his younger brother, but it was the first time he'd ever been so detailed in describing something about him. Cid resisted the urge to look up at Alex, sensing that while it was a pivotal moment, it was also a little bit of a private one.

"He was right," Cid told him, running his hand over Alex's leg. "I could go anywhere with you around, and I'd feel completely safe and taken care of. It's just something about you."

"I think he would have really liked you," Alex said softly. "You would have probably got along really well. Though you both would've driven me nuts. Both of you together, with all that energy, constantly happy all the time?"

Cid chuckled. "It would have been torture for you."

Alex snorted. "Yeah, a little. But it would have been alright too. He was always keeping me from getting too serious or going 'too dark' as he always put it. I might've been the one making sure the bills were paid and the groceries were bought, but he was the one who kept me going sometimes, kept me sane."

"You took care of each other," Cid said softly.

"Yeah, I guess we did. Didn't think I would have someone else in my life who could do that for me. But the more I hang out with you, the more I get to thinkin' that maybe, just maybe, I might've found it again."

There was pain in the other man's voice, but there was a note of warmth and happiness there too. Cid imagined it was probably quite bittersweet to be reminiscing about his brother while also talking about his time with Cid. Honestly, Cid didn't know how the man could do it, see enough of his brother in Cid while still managing to be around him.

"You're a strong man, Alex," Cid told him softly, closing his eyes. "I hope you know that."

"I hope I'm strong enough," Alex said, so quiet that Cid almost didn't catch the words.

There wasn't much he could say to that, though, but he kept his grip on Alex. Sometimes all a person could do is simply be there, existing as something for them to hold onto and bear them through the hard times.

ALEX

Day Thirteen

ALEX PUSHED the front door to his apartment closed with a soft kick, rolling his eyes as he held his new phone up to his ear. There had been no way in hell he was going to go without a cell phone, not as far as his handlers were concerned. At least the purchase of the new phone had gone on Uncle Sam's card instead of his own.

"Yeah, Ken, I know," Alex told the agent.

"Do you? Because it doesn't sound like you do," Ken said, sounding irritated. "You're supposed to be keeping your head down."

"And what? Hide away in my apartment when I'm not at work? Just not talk to people? Don't have a life?" Alex growled back at him, tossing his keys angrily down on the table beside the door. "That's bullshit."

"There's a difference between having a social life and having a dating life. Relationships don't tend to survive witness protection," Ken informed him. "It's not like you can tell him much about your life, not unless you want to risk giving away your identity."

There was no way in hell Alex was going to offer up what he had told Cid so far. Knowing his luck, it was probably too much and the agent, who was probably a helicopter parent, would have swooped down in an instant to move him. Alex didn't think he'd told Cid enough for there to be a concern but he also trusted that Cid wasn't going to dig too deeply either. If the man had wanted to take a peek, he probably could have done so already, and any search for information would have alerted Ken and his team.

"You're being dramatic," Alex said, kicking his boots off. "It's not a big deal."

"You getting yourself a boyfriend is a big deal. It's a potential breach."

"He's not my boyfriend," Alex corrected, though he wondered if that was going to stay true for much longer. It wasn't as if he and Cid were making any attempts to keep a 'safe' distance between them. "We're seeing each other. Calm down."

"And what if something happens? If your identity is compromised?" Ken demanded to know.

Alex stopped, looking around the living room and frowning. For a moment, he would have sworn that he'd smelled something light and flowery. The more he looked around the room, the more he felt his nerves tighten. Nothing seemed out of place, but the entire room suddenly felt a little too poorly lit and foreboding for his taste.

"Alex, are you listening to me?" Ken said sharply.

Alex rolled his eyes. "He's not going to compromise me. I haven't told him anything that he needs to worry about, or you, alright?"

Which was true...probably.

Ken continued as Alex cautiously moved through the small apartment. "And if you're wrong? Or what if someone does find you. Who do you think they're going to go for? You, or him?"

Alex stopped short. "That's not funny."

"I wasn't trying to be."

"And it's not fucking fair either. You damn well know how I would feel about that after what happened to Rio."

"Exactly. I'm trying to make a point. Not be an asshole."

"Funny how they sound like the same thing."

Ken sighed. "Look, I can't stop you, and really, it's not even against the rules. What I'm saying is, be careful, and be smart, alright? I don't want you or anyone innocent to get hurt, and that's my biggest concern."

"Thanks. I got that," Alex growled.

The remainder of the conversation was brief and curt, and Alex was more than happy to get off the phone. He flopped onto his couch, half-tempted to break the damn thing and make Ken and his team pay for a new one all over again.

Alex knew there were dangers, but that didn't mean he was being stupid about it. They were hours away from Port Dale, and no one would ever suspect that he would come to some quiet little college town to get away. He hadn't told Cid about anything significant, and no one but Ken's team knew where he was at. Worried or not, Ken had delivered a low blow and the reminder of his brother had only served to foul up Alex's mood.

Which was precisely why when his phone buzzed again, Alex was ready to chuck it out the nearest window. Instead, he grabbed it up from the couch, ready to tell Ken to fuck off if it was him.

Instead, it was a picture of Cid, or rather, from Cid's

phone. Cid was mid-jump in the picture, a look of extreme concentration on his face. His arms were outstretched before him, apparently intent on something that was out of shot.

Below it was a message.

This is where you've chosen to lay your affections btw. He's trying to catch a butterfly.

Below that was another message.

Alice took my phone. I didn't catch it. :(

Alex grinned at his phone, tapping out a quick message back.

You're an idiot.

Yeah, but I'm kinda your idiot.

"Yeah," Alex said fondly, running the side of his finger over the picture. "You kind of are."

DAY FIFTEEN

ALEX WOULD SWEAR up and down that entering Cid was unlike fucking anyone else.

Despite being in a supply closet, just off a hallway where anyone could hear them, Cid let out a groan. Alex had no choice but to slap his hand over the man's mouth, gripping his face tightly as he pushed another inch into him. Truth be told, it was difficult to keep himself quiet as Cid's body greeted him happily, allowing him to push into the warm depths of the man's body with the pleasant grip he was becoming obsessed with.

It was supposed to be a simple lunch date. The two of them meeting for an hour with the food Cid had ordered while they sat and ate in a relatively quiet hallway in the Science building. It wasn't like they wouldn't have had time for some fun after work or even a good chunk of the weekend when Cid wasn't scheduled to work.

Instead, Alex had found himself dragging Cid into the nearest supply closet. Though 'dragging' might not have been the right word since Cid had not only come willingly, but it had been his hands working their way down the front of Alex's pants that had started the entire ordeal in the first place. That and it had been Cid who had come with both lube and condoms for what should have been a perfectly innocent lunch together.

Cid's next moan vibrated against Alex's palm. Apparently, the man was taking the impromptu gag as a sign that he was perfectly okay to make as much noise as he wanted. As much as Alex was tempted to warn him that Cid was loud when he wanted to be, he was quickly getting to the point where he didn't care. Hell, the supply closet was out of the way, and the nearby hall was one of the least used in the building. Maybe they could afford to be a little ballsy.

Which was around the point that Alex drove himself, balls deep, into the other man. Cid shuddered, pushing back against him as he reached down to wrap his hand around his own straining cock. They hadn't done much more than shove their pants down to the middle of their thighs, which was just far enough for Alex to hear the sharp crack of skin meeting skin as he shoved himself once more into Cid.

This wasn't meant to last long, and Alex knew it. Their bodies crashed together as he buried himself time and time again inside of Cid, groaning softly into the man's neck as he fucked him from behind. Cid's legs were spread wide, allowing Alex perfect access, though they began to shake and threatened to buckle as Alex drove into him again and again.

That was no problem for Alex, who wrapped a thick arm around Cid's waist, bending the man over onto the nearby shelf and shoved in once again. It was becoming increasingly difficult to keep themselves upright, but he could sense the tautness in the other man's body, feel his pleasure and excitement as it shuddered through him.

When Cid came, it was with a cry, barely muffled by Alex's hand against his mouth. His whole body shuddered, bearing down fiercely around Alex's cock. And not unlike their first time, Alex forced himself to pull out from the other man, yanking off the condom to toss aside and giving his cock a few vigorous strokes. With a groan that could probably be heard by anyone who was nearby, he splattered the man's bare ass with his cum, hips bucking as he did so.

"Shit," Cid chuckled, sagging against the shelving unit he'd been trying to use as a handhold. "What did you do?"

"Made a mess of you," Alex said fondly, pushing a finger up inside of Cid with a grin. "Which you love."

Cid's hips buckled. "God, don't. Why does that still feel good?"

"Because, just like me, you're a bit of a slut," Alex said fondly.

"A slut for you," Cid said, affection in his tone as well.

And just like that, Alex felt his own internal equilibrium shift at those very simple words. He knew it was likely Cid had been just as free and open with others in the past, but those people were in the past. In the present, however, Cid had chosen him for this, had wanted to be expressive and uninhibited with Alex.

Because he trusted Alex. Because he felt safe with Alex.

"Damn right," Alex growled, barely managing to hold back the shake in his voice.

Cid turned on the spot, not caring that he was barely able to stand or that his ass was covered in Alex's cum. He wrapped his arms around Alex's neck and kissed him, managing to somehow both be heated and content at the same time.

"I might be turning you into a romantic," Cid teased in a low voice, nibbling gently on Alex's lower lip.

"Maybe," Alex admitted, knowing there was no point in denying what was apparently a blatant truth. "But that doesn't mean I'm not going to fuck you sideways."

"Ooh," Cid said in a mocking scandalized voice. "Are you saying you're going to fuck me like a whore?"

"Fuck you like a whore," Alex agreed, kissing him quickly. "And kiss you like a prince."

Cid laughed, his cheeks coloring. "I could get used to that."

"Good," Alex told him fondly. "Now, let's get dressed before someone actually finds us. That'll be awkward."

Cid did so, hiking up his pants without a care in the world that he was probably soaking his underwear with Alex's cum. Instead, his eyes were bright and locked onto Alex. His face, his hands, and just the general movement of his body. For his own part, Alex was watching him just as intently, content to just be with Cid, even if it was in a cramped, somewhat dirty supply closet after having nailed the man against the nearest shelving unit.

"You are getting sappy on me," Cid said fondly before opening the door and disappearing out into the hallway.

Alex shrugged, knowing it was probably true and not even bothering to care before he followed Cid out into the hallway, a small smile on his face.

DAY **Eighteen**

"WHAT ARE you smiling at over there?" Cid asked from his spot on his living room chair.

"My phone," Alex told him, looking over the edge of his device. "Why you bein' so nosy?"

"Why are you being so evasive?"

"Because you're being nosy."

"Which is because you're avoiding the question."

Alex rolled his eyes, refusing to take the bait any further and continuing the mock argument between them. He knew Cid had enough energy and determination to continue it, long past the point of patience for Alex.

He had always heard Sundays were supposed to be lazy days, but it turned out Saturdays were just as good for that. Alex's schedule had always allowed him to have the week-ends to himself unless he'd been feeling bored enough to go into work. Cid however, worked whenever he was needed, and that need could shift throughout the week. They'd both known the man would have Friday and Saturday off, and after Alex had left his Friday shift, the two of them had been together ever since.

It should have been a little strange, spending so much time with another person as he'd done over the past couple of weeks. Yet, just as he'd told Cid a time or two, there was something ultimately comfortable and soothing about being around the other man. Cid had by no means somehow transformed Alex into a grinning idiot. Alex fondly considered that to be Cid's role. But there was no denying that being around Cid had made Alex the happiest he'd been since his brother had died.

"I'm looking at old pictures," Alex finally told him, sliding over to another picture.

"Anything good?" Cid asked, glancing up from the screen where he was mindlessly mowing down what Alex thought were either monsters or demons.

"Pictures of Rio and I," Alex said with a shrug.

There was a silence between them then, and Alex didn't know if it was because Cid was wrapped up in what he was doing or because he was trying to think of what to say. The other man had always been incredibly cautious and respectful whenever Rio had been brought up. Alex thought it was pretty obvious that Cid wanted to ask plenty of questions but always held himself back despite that.

"When you're done," Alex told him, now looking at the screen Cid was playing on. "You can come over here and take a peek since I know you're burning to see."

"I'm not burning to see," Cid protested even as he paused the game and pushed up from his chair.

"Right, because you didn't just stop your slaughter of living things to come over here," Alex snorted.

"Why do you have to make it sound so ugly?"

"You're literally massacring a bunch of ugly dudes to the sounds of death metal. What else am I supposed to make it sound like?"

"Something interesting and cool?"

"Plus, aren't you a doctor? Don't you have to like, swear to do no harm?"

Cid plopped down next to him with a huff. "That doesn't apply to demons from a hell dimension trying to take over and destroy ours. I think we're allowed to whip out the shotguns and grenades for that one."

"Good to know," Alex said with a snort, holding his phone out for Cid to see.

He'd started with the one that had been his lock screen since he'd taken it. There he and Rio were, standing among the lights of Port Dale's boardwalk, bright drink in Rio's hand, and a stupid grin on both of their faces.

"God," Cid said with a smile. "Even if you hadn't told me, I would have known you guys were brothers."

"He was like, half my size," Alex pointed out.

"Yeah but," Cid waved his finger at the screen as though that would somehow clarify his point. "There's things that are the same. You might be half-giant, but you can see the similarities. In the eyes, the shape of the nose, and though you don't pull it out as much, you've got the same happy smile as him too."

"It was a good night," Alex admitted. "He was hopped up on that stupid drink that tasted like pure fucking sugar. And he'd spent way too much money on some carnival game just to win this weird-looking stuffed cat, but it was a good night."

Cid laughed at that. "Well, it looks like a good night."

It was nice to share, even if it did bring on the familiar sharp clench in his chest as he stared down at his brother's happy expression.

"He was the only person who knew I was into guys too," Alex told him softly.

"Oh yeah?"

"Yeah. People we grew up around...well, they would've been pissed if they'd found out. I never told anyone before Rio, hell, I wasn't even trying to tell Rio. But he came home early from school one day, something about a mercury spill or whatever. Our mom was out getting her latest fix, and I had a guy over."

Alex had thought his heart was going to lodge itself permanently in his chest when Rio barged through the front door. The two brothers had stared at one another, Rio's eyes going huge, and Alex forgetting to breathe. The guy he'd been pinning to the couch beneath him was just as confused but remained quiet the whole time.

"Rio thought it was fucking hilarious," Alex told him with a soft chuckle. "Told me the look on my face when he saw us was gonna rank up there as one of his favorites."

"I guess he didn't care all that much, huh?" Cid asked softly.

Alex shook his head. "No. He told me he didn't care who I was banging or dated. I was still who I was before that. He knew why I kept it quiet, but he was glad he got to find out. All he cared about was that he could tease me for almost shitting my pants after he found me and the guy."

"I'm sure it was a pretty funny look," Cid said.

"Probably," Alex said, staring at the picture.

"I'm glad he didn't care," Cid told him, laying his head on Alex's shoulder.

"I should have known better," Alex said, flipping to another picture of them holding up two cones of ice cream while standing on the street. "Rio was...always different than everyone else. I don't know how he did it, growing up where we did, but he always stayed happy and smiling, always trying to see the best in people."

"Probably helped to have someone like you there in his life," Cid told him, nuzzling against him.

"Sometimes it felt like all I did was try to keep him alive," Alex admitted.

"Maybe that was the case sometimes, but it's obvious you have nothing but love for him. And people are going to notice that. Like I said before, you took care of each other.

And with someone like you taking care of him, I can imagine he grew up feeling pretty happy and safe," Cid told him.

Alex looked askance at Cid, searching his face. "You really have that high an opinion of me?"

Cid chuckled, blue eyes sparkling as they gazed up at Alex. "Absolutely. It can be hard sometimes to see how we really are, mostly because we live in our own heads. But you're a good man, Alex, and you've obviously got a big heart too. I'm starting to feel more and more lucky to have someone like you in my life, giving me a chance to have the time we've had."

"It isn't about luck," Alex told him, setting his phone on his lap. "How could I not want someone like you in my life? I kind of forgot what it was like to feel okay with things, to not just...do life instead of having one. But the last few weeks have been...something else, and that's because of you."

"I'm glad," Cid said warmly, smiling that wonderful smile of his.

Alex kissed him then, pulling the man closer to him as he enjoyed Cid's body pressing against his. If it wasn't for the fact that having a relationship, a true one, with Cid would feel dishonest, he would have happily asked the man for something more than what they had. If that meant slapping a label on it, then so be it, so long as they got to be one another's.

And before he could push the temptation away, Cid uttered something that froze Alex in place.

"I think I'm falling for you."

CID

As soon as the words left his mouth, Cid knew he'd said the wrong thing. The languid feel of Alex's body immediately became taut. The man sucked in a breath, held it, and from where Cid had his head laying near the man's chest, he could hear the sudden heavy thumping of the man's chest in the quiet of the living room.

"Uh," Alex began, his voice shaking at the edges.

Cid winced, knowing he'd pushed things too far. Unable to bear the feeling of tension in the man's body anymore, Cid pushed away from him. He was a little surprised to find that Alex's reaction was completely expected. Neither of them had talked about anything that came close to a true commitment. And while Alex had never blatantly avoided the topic, he'd never tried to broach it either.

"Sorry," Cid said, feeling his chest tighten at the word. "It just kind of...slipped out."

Alex grimaced, setting his phone aside to turn toward Cid. "No, it's...I wasn't expecting it, that was all."

Cid watched him, trying to gauge the emotions he could catch going across Alex's face. How hadn't the man figured out what was happening by now? Or was it that Alex had been purposefully avoiding seeing what was happening? Cid had hoped the past few weeks or so had been enough to slowly turn things around, maybe open the door to doing more than just seeing if there was something there and actually committing to it.

"I don't really know what to say," Cid admitted with a listless shrug.

Alex looked pained, and for a moment, Cid felt a stab of guilt in his gut. They'd been having a moment of happiness, with Alex opening up a little more and talking about a potentially painful subject. Then Cid had turned around and let his mouth get ahead of him, and suddenly they were both sitting there, staring at each other awkwardly.

"Don't get that look on your face," Alex said, wrinkling his nose. "You look like a puppy who just piddled on the rug."

Cid couldn't even summon his usual ability to laugh at something ridiculous. "Kind of feels like I did."

Alex shook his head, hand twitching toward Cid and then stilling. "No. You didn't do anything wrong, okay? It's just...it's complicated."

"Because of the stuff you can't tell me?" Cid guessed.

Alex looked down at his lap, nodding slowly. "Trust me, I want to tell you. I've thought about it, a lot."

Cid decided now was the time to ask the question he'd been holding back for quite some time. "Then why don't you?"

Alex sighed heavily. "Because..."

"It's complicated," Cid supplied, unable to keep the bitterness out of his voice.

Alex winced but nodded. "Look, if I told you why I can't tell you, then I might as well be telling you the whole thing. But not telling you just feels fucked up because I like being around you. I like doing things with you. So it feels like lying."

"Can't really call it lying when you've been honest about not being able to tell me things since early on," Cid pointed out, still believing that.

"Maybe. Still feels like it. And I mean, who the fuck can enter a whole ass relationship with someone when they know they're not going to tell them a big something? Having a big ass secret sit between us doesn't sound like a good idea," Alex said, fidgeting now.

"Maybe," Cid said slowly, thinking he understood where Alex's hesitation was coming from. "Or maybe not. I still don't think it was lying or that you would be lying. Before we ever started dating a little more seriously, you told me you couldn't tell me everything. That's pretty honest. And I was still okay with it, which is my choice."

Alex shook his head, pushing off of the couch. "You shouldn't have to be okay with it. That ain't right."

"It's still my choice to make," Cid insisted. "I can make choices for myself, you know."

Alex spun around, eyes narrowing. "I'm not saying that because you're some little kid who I think I need to babysit. But there's shit about me you don't even know, and I do know it. So it feels like I'm doing you dirty by keeping it to myself."

"Is it bad?" Cid asked, not sure how he'd feel if the answer was yes.

Alex hesitated, and Cid thought that was enough of an answer right there.

"It ain't pretty," Alex said softly, turning away as though he knew Cid was reading his expressions.

"Alex," Cid began, then stopped when he realized he didn't know what he wanted to say.

Once more, Alex shook his head, grabbing his phone off the table and stuffing it into his pants. "Look, I knew this shit was gonna come up one day, but I guess I wasn't ready for it just yet. I need to think about shit, get my head on straight."

"You're leaving?" Cid asked faintly, his chest aching once again.

Alex glanced back at him, face expressionless. "I have to. After this? No way I can sit around and pretend everything's like it was, and I...no, I can't talk about it right now. I don't even know what to fucking think."

Cid felt helpless as he watched Alex grab his jacket and start putting on his shoes. There was no way he could force the man to stay, nor would he want to. But he couldn't help feeling like Alex walking away wasn't the answer, and would do nothing but hurt whatever they might be able to salvage between them if things were going to keep crashing and burning.

"Look," Alex began, stopping at the front door. "I'll text you, alright? But I need to...to think, get some air. Make up my fucking mind, okay? I'm sorry, Cid, I really fucking am."

And then he was gone, and Cid was left in the quiet of his house, wondering about how quickly everything could collapse in a matter of seconds.

"AND THEN HE just walked out, just like that?" Alice asked, popping a chip into her mouth and chewing thoughtfully.

They were at their favorite spot just outside the clinic. It was a warm Sunday afternoon, and despite the sunlight bathing them, Cid barely noticed it. He was miserable. He knew it, Alice knew it, and he suspected anyone who met him would probably know it at a glance. Cid had never been very good at concealing his emotions, mostly because he rarely tried to. Alice had taken one look at him when she'd shown up for a Sunday lunch and immediately demanded to know what had happened.

"Yeah, just like that," Cid informed her, mindlessly plucking blades of grass.

Cid hadn't tried to contact Alex after the man had left. Instead, he lazed around the living room feeling sorry for himself until he had to crawl into bed. Where he had promptly felt bad for himself until falling asleep, only to wake up still miserable. It wasn't often that he couldn't find some spark of joy or some sliver of hope in a situation, but he was struggling to keep his head held high.

"That's either some serious commitment issues," Alice said, choosing another chip from the crinkling bag. "Or he was straight up telling you the truth."

Cid glanced at her. "Oh what, now you believe he might not be a liar?"

Alice shrugged. "I still said it could be commitment issues, which means he could be lying. But like you said, he might not be lying."

"You were pretty sure before."

"I was sure when you two were first starting out and having fun. But you guys have been going at it for a few weeks now. If he was just going to play, wouldn't he have had his fun and run by now?"

Cid shrugged, not sure if that was the case or not. He'd never really dealt with a player before, so he didn't know how they operated. Generally speaking, if someone wasn't interested, either they'd let him know when it happened, or Cid figured it out and ended it before it dragged on too long. For all he knew, Alex had been in it for the long con, enjoying what he was getting but always keeping the exit door in sight.

He didn't believe that was the case, but he had to privately admit it was possible.

"Maybe he's like, some badass assassin," Alice offered up, oh so helpfully. "Or like, a prince in some other country, on the run from people trying to kill him."

Cid squinted over at her. "You really need to stop reading those crazy books."

She tossed her hair over one shoulder with a snort. "You know I can't read."

Cid rolled his eyes. Alice was one of the most voracious readers he'd ever seen in his life. She wasn't particularly picky about genre either. The woman could tear through a gory horror novel just as enthusiastically as he could through a gentle romance.

"I'm making a joke to make a serious point," Alice told him.

"Well, I missed the serious point."

"Maybe he's telling you the truth. Maybe there is a perfectly good reason he can't tell you...whatever it is that he can't tell you," Alice said. "You don't have to only read fiction books to know that sometimes people can't talk about certain things. Do you think the spouses of federal agents get to hear everything that happens on the job? Do you think therapists tell their families what they have to listen to every day at work? People have to live with and love people that can't tell them everything all the time."

"I mean, that's pretty much what I told him," Cid pointed out.

"Sort of, but sort of not too. You were so freaked out by his reaction and worried about what he was going to say. I think you probably just did the rambling thing you do. Where you just...vomit out every thought in your head."

"It wasn't that bad, I mean it."

"Maybe not, but I doubt you phrased it logically and reasonably."

"Well," Cid begrudged. "I did kind of tell him it was my choice to make, not his."

"Which, while true, is also not the most compelling argument to hear when you're trying to make up your mind about whether or not you're doing the right thing by another person," Alice pointed out.

"If he's telling me the truth in the first place," Cid said, reminding her of her own skeptical stance.

Alice shrugged. "Look, either you break things down to him and talk them out, like adults with healthy communication skills should, or you let him brood while you walk around like you've been gut-shot."

Cid scowled at her. "You're a terrible friend. I haven't..."

"Yes, you have."

"Terrible."

"And also the truth. Just like it's the truth that after you get off work, you should go talk to him."

"Shouldn't I wait until he's ready to talk?"

Alice shrugged once more. "Maybe, and someone else might tell you to wait. I'm not an expert on people you know. But from the sounds of it, you two have some shit to hash out. All you can do is try to see if he's willing to talk through things right now with a little push from you. If not, you wait. If he takes forever, then it's probably a good idea to just let him go. Because if he's not ready to talk soon, he's never going to be."

"And what am I supposed to say?" Cid asked helplessly.

"Think about what you mean, put it into words, and then go say those words to him. Let him talk, but make sure you're heard. And then figure out what the hell is going to happen next. If he's playing games, drop him so fast it makes his head spin. If he's being serious, then try to figure things out. If he still can't stomach going through with a relationship while keeping a secret, then you'll have to let him go."

"There's a whole lot of opportunity for him and me to just...end in your little scenario there," Cid pointed out, feeling a little queasy.

Alice shot him a sympathetic look. "I know, sweetie, I know. But you know better than anyone that life doesn't always go the way we want it to or wish it would. But if you ask me, you shouldn't just let things drop. Even if this has all been one big game, at the very least, you deserve to know the truth."

Cid chuckled. "The difference between being dragged into a fight to the death or walking in with my head held high?"

"Or the difference between being alone or having someone at your side. Because hey, who knows, this might actually be something worth having."

Cid plucked another piece of grass thoughtfully. "I guess there's only one way to find out."

"Bingo," Alice said with a snort. "Now, can I go back to

making fun of you? All this sweetness and love is starting to make my teeth ache."

"Okay, woman who's fond of romance novels," Cid said with a grin. "Whatever you say."

———

BY THE TIME his shift ended, Cid was almost sure about what he wanted to say when he finally faced Alex. Once he was clocked out, he contemplated texting Alex and finding out if the man would meet him face to face. Yet, he held back, thinking that a text would offer one too many avenues of escape or evasion. And maybe it was a little too forward or pushy to go to the man's house and confront him there, but Cid thought he might as well take Alice's advice as far as it could go and talk to him face to face.

He had never been to Alex's apartment in person before, but a week ago he'd managed to wriggle the address out of the man. Cid had ordered some novelty socks and a new phone case for him to have sent to his house. Cid would have had it sent to his own home, but packages had a tendency to get lost when sent to his house, and he thought it would be simpler to have the gifts sent to Alex directly instead of Cid's usual delivery destination which was Alice's apartment. Plus, he still got the annoyed text from Alex when he'd opened the packages and found socks with adorable bunnies all over them and a phone case with a cartoon sea urchin on it, equipped with a speech bubble that had simply said 'I need a hug.'

Alex's apartment building was on the far edge of town. There, Greenford got a little more rundown, but Cid thought it was still beautiful in its own way. He remembered learning that it had been the place where Greenford had started, many decades before, growing outward into what was Greenford proper. Once newer and nicer buildings started becoming the face of Greenford, the older, slightly more rundown buildings were used for lower-income housing.

Cid got out of his car after parking, looking around the small collection of buildings that served as an apartment complex. The grass patches around the buildings were kept neat, and some of the apartments had well-maintained gardens, with flowers and a few herbs growing in window boxes or pots.

When he found Alex's apartment, it had none of the little decorations or added touches that some of the apartments had. There wasn't even a mat outside the door. While he knew Alex wasn't exactly the gardening type, it still struck him as a little odd that there was no personalization whatsoever.

Shaking off the feeling of strangeness, he reached out and stopped. The door wasn't completely closed. It was open just enough for Cid to see the door frame and a slit of darkness from the apartment.

He stood there for a moment, unsure what to do. That the door was open a crack wasn't all that weird. Greenford wasn't known for its high crime rate, and people were occasionally lax about security. For all he knew, Alex had gone out to get his mail and had just not closed the door carefully behind him.

What struck him as odd was the fact that it was dark inside. The sun had set half an hour before, and from inside, Cid could see no lights were on, not even the TV. Why would Alex be sitting around in the dark?

The uneasy feeling in his stomach grew stronger as he reached for the doorknob and stopped once again. Shaking his head, he turned away from the door, reaching into his pocket to pull out his phone. First, he was going to call Alex and find out where he was, and if he wasn't at his apartment, then they could figure it out. Something was off, and Cid didn't want to go into the man's apartment by himself in case someone who shouldn't be in there was.

His phone lit up as he unlocked it, and once again, he hesitated. What if someone had already gone into the apartment, and Alex was in there alone and injured. Cid winced at the thought, knowing full well if there was anyone well-equipped to find someone injured, it would be him.

The door behind him creaked, ending his thoughts as he turned. Before he could register what he was seeing, strong hands grabbed him by the shoulders and yanked him back and off his feet. His back hit the ground, knocking the air from his lungs with a harsh gust of breath. Before he had time to recover, however, pain lanced up the side of his face, knocking what sense he had left in him and sending the room spinning, darkness hovering at the edge of his vision.

A sharp female voice cut through his haze. "You fucking idiots. That's not him."

A low voice rumbled in return and the woman growled. "That's the fucking boy toy."

Cid struggled to get his head to cooperate with him, freezing when he heard a low, unfamiliar male speak. "So what, do we just kill him and wait?"

Cid's heart thumped ferociously in his chest in the silence, waiting for the answer.

"No," the woman said, sounding thoughtful. "This'll work. We're leaving. Grab this idiot. We'll take him back to the office. We can just make Rico come to us."

Cid had no idea what was going on, but he knew enough to know he wasn't going to be immediately killed.

Taken against his will, yes, but not killed. Somehow, he didn't think that was a whole lot better and he needed to get away from them if he had any chance of surviving.

"He's still moving," the man said, sounding amused. "Little fag's got a hard head."

"So hit him again and let's go," the woman snarled.

Cid knew a bright, hot pain once more, and then only darkness.

ALEX

Alex was quickly beginning to regret taking on an extra shift. When he'd called Archy and offered to come in, it had sounded like a great idea. If it meant not having to sit around his apartment by himself, feeling like absolute shit, then he would take the opportunity. And yeah, it was going to be a late shift, which would suck when he had to roll back in on Monday morning early, but it beat stewing in his own misery.

But he was beginning to get a headache, one that didn't want to go away. Add to that, it hadn't done much to alleviate his mood in the slightest. Especially at the beginning of the shift, when he knew that Cid was only about a ten-minute walk away, probably just as unhappy if not more, while in the clinic. For the first few hours, his job had been less of a distraction and more a constant battle not to go talk to the man.

Thing was, Alex didn't know what he would even say to Cid. Ken had been right. Telling Cid the truth might end up putting him in danger, more so than being with Cid already was. At the same time, Alex couldn't stand the idea of keeping important things from Cid, even if the man was more than willing to put up with it. There was nothing fair about it in Alex's mind, and the war between what he wanted and what he felt was right kept going on in his head.

A groan escaped him as he bent over to grab one of his spray bottles. The vibration of his phone in his pocket was the last thing he wanted. There were only two people who would conceivably call him. There was no way he was in the mood to talk to Ken, and he had no idea what the hell he was supposed to say if it was Cid.

With a grimace, he pulled out his phone, chest tightening when he saw Cid's name and face on the screen. Alex had grabbed a picture of the man while he'd been gaming one evening. Cid had been so engrossed in the game, he hadn't even noticed, hunched forward, eyes wide, and his tongue sticking out between his lips as he tried to best whatever monster he was fighting at the time.

Knowing there was no way he could ever purposefully avoid Cid, he answered the call with a sigh. "Hey, look…"

A female voice interrupted. "Hello, Rico."

Alex froze, hand gripping the phone fiercely. The use of his former name, his real name, left him feeling as though he'd been splashed with icy water. Not only that, but some part of his brain knew that voice, though he couldn't immediately place it.

"Who is this?" he asked slowly, gripping the phone so hard he thought it might snap. "And why do you have Cid's phone?"

"Oh, is that his name?" she asked, sounding amused. "He wouldn't tell us. Probably wouldn't have given us the phone either, but well, people and their technology. All we needed was his finger."

"You had better not have hurt him," Alex growled,

imagining all the horrible things that could have happened to Cid from just that one statement. "I'll fucking end you."

She laughed, the sound high and cruel. "We haven't hurt him...much. Nothing he can't walk away from eventually. But if you want him to stay that way, you're going to listen very carefully to me, you got it?"

"I'm listening," Alex told her, mind frantically trying to figure out what to do next.

"There's a building, about a half-hour past the city limits. Old factory, practically falling apart, you can't miss it. Meet us there."

"And then?"

"And then, it's simple. You, for him. You show up in the next hour, and he gets to walk away scot-free."

"It'll take longer than that to get there," Alex protested, thinking of trying to get off campus and out of town in that amount of time.

"Not my problem. But you'd better be quick. I'd really hate to have to hurt him even more. One hour."

The line clicked off and Alex swore vehemently. He was just shy of chucking the phone, and then realized he might need it. There was absolutely no time for him to call the police or Ken and expect them to mobilize fast enough. Especially because the time limit required that he show up, and he had no doubt the woman had meant for him to show up by himself.

Still, while he didn't want to risk Cid's life even more, he didn't want to leave both of them out to dry. He tossed the spray bottle in his hand aside and opened up his message thread with Ken.

Sending address soon. Be there as quick as possible. Be quiet, but bring guns. There's an innocent there.

It was by far the most precise and well-worded text he

thought he'd ever sent. Some distant part of his brain found it amusing that it took a life-or-death situation to make it happen, especially since he was sprinting across the campus to get to his car. By the time he reached it, he had pulled up the map for Greenford, and found the only factory within reasonable driving distance of the town limits.

"Please let this be the right choice," Alex said softly as he threw himself into the driver's seat and sent the address to Ken. "Please, please."

THE ONLY THING Alex was thankful for as he drove up into the parking lot of the decrepit-looking factory was that there had been no cops on the road. Alex had pushed his poor, rundown car as hard as it could go to make it past the town limits and into the thick woods that lined the major roads in and out of Greenford.

The caller had been right. There was no way in hell he would have missed the factory if he was driving by it. The smokestacks towered over even the highest trees, and the roof of the tallest building was visible from the road. It wasn't one of the biggest factories he'd ever seen and would probably still be considered small by the standards of Port Dale.

And she had been right about it practically falling apart. There didn't seem to be a window in the place that wasn't broken or at least horribly cracked. Deep crevices had arched their way down the part of the building Alex suspected had been used for shipping, and while there might have been a brick facade at one point, it had crumbled to dust, leaving dark smears on the concrete face of the building.

Once he was parked, he took one look at his phone, knowing there was no point in bringing it inside with him. There were a few texts from Ken demanding to know what was happening and where Alex was. Sighing, he locked his phone, knowing its contents, particularly the SOS message to Ken, were safe from being seen. Unlike Cid, Alex didn't use the fingerprint option on his phone, and he doubted they would waste time trying to unlock his phone when they already had him in their clutches.

Stepping out of the car, he looked around the cracked and crumbling parking lot. The nearest entrance was a set of double doors on the front of the shortest part of the building. From the look of the collection of windows, he guessed that had been the administration block, where the office workers had done their jobs. It was also the only door that had a light over it, flickering and dim, but on.

Just as he began to approach it, the doors swung open and two men walked out. They weren't nearly as big as him, but they weren't shy about showing the guns at their side or on their backs either.

"Guess you're my welcome," Alex said, looking between them.

One of them jerked his head toward the doors. "C'mon, and don't get stupid."

Alex rolled his eyes and did as he was told, with each man flanking him. He wasn't going to do anything at all while they had Cid somewhere. He might be willing to risk his own life to survive, but he wasn't going to get Cid killed when none of this should have been his problem in the first place.

They led him into the building and at a glance, he saw that he was right. Old desks, covered in heavy dust and cobwebs, some broken or falling apart, lay scattered around the main floor. The men led him not into the factory itself but up a set of stairs that creaked dangerously as they made their way up. The second floor wasn't much different than the first, save that a room at the end of the hall was lit up, the door ajar.

He didn't need the harsh nudge from one of the men behind him to know where they expected him to go. Alex stepped through the door and found that the room was a little cleaner than the rest, though still rundown. A large metal desk sat in the middle. Behind it was the only chair, and it was occupied.

"Hello, Rico," Sofia De La Cruz said, grinning widely at the sight of him.

Now Alex realized why the voice on the phone had sounded so familiar. Sofia De La Cruz just so happened to be the younger half-sister of the current head of the Los Muertos, Antonio. More so than Antonio's full-blooded siblings, she was pretty heavily involved in the day-to-day business of the gang. Hers was a face that he would have seen on occasion, though not often enough that it would have immediately stood out in a crowd.

"Sofia," Alex said softly. "Your brother's got you doing his dirty work all the way out here?"

"You shouldn't even be out here," she sneered. "You should be back in Port Dale, doing what you're supposed to be doing. Instead, you're hiding out here like a rat, holing up with some pretty boy, and pretending like you didn't stab us in the back."

"Fuck you," Alex snarled at her. "We had a deal. You fuckers broke it. I don't owe you shit anymore."

"You could have just walked away, Rico," she told him, shaking her head. "Walked away and left us alone. But no, you had to go to the Feds. You had to know we wouldn't let you go after that."

"Liar," Alex shot back. "I'd been helping you guys for years. Sure, I wasn't the one pushing the shit, offing assholes, or sitting in your meetings, but I knew shit. I knew a lot of shit, and you would've never let me get away. Never."

Sofia snorted softly but didn't bother to refute him. They both knew Alex had collected quite a lot of information on the Los Muertos, where they operated, the different ways they operated, who was who, who did what, when they did it. Just by simply being in the background, a meathead, there to protect some asshole or scare the fuck out of someone else, but one who had seen enough to cause a lot of trouble for them if they started talking.

He looked around the room, noting again that it had been cleaned up. And he was reminded of the light outside, as well as the one barely keeping the room lit hanging over the desk.

"You've been here for a little while, haven't you?" Alex guessed, wondering just how long.

Sofia curled her lip. "Wasn't hard to find you once we started digging. You know we don't just work outta the Dale. But since you went running to the Feds, we had to be careful about getting our hands on ya. Didn't need to give them a reason to come after us."

"So you've been watching me," Alex said, feeling an ugly twist in his stomach at the thought.

Just how much had they seen?

"Didn't want pigs on us, so we were careful. Tried to get you outta your safehouse, which didn't work," Sofia said with a roll of her eyes. "Shoulda worked too, but your pretty boy got in the way."

Alex straightened at that, remembering the night. "You! You were the drunk woman!"

Sofia smirked. "I've been told I'm a pretty good actress when I wanna be. Was banking on the fact that you wouldn't know me right away, not while you were distracted and in a club."

"You fucking drugged me?" Alex asked, unable to help his indignation. "With a date rape drug?"

"Don't worry, baby," she assured him in a soft coo. "You might have turned into a cock hungry homo when you turned your back on us, but all my boys know the right team to swing for. We wouldn't have raped you. Probably would've wished we had by the time we were done with you, but not rape."

Alex ground his teeth, annoyed that she had been around for weeks and no one, not even him, had noticed. Apparently, it hadn't been such a good idea to distance himself from Ken.

"The car was clumsy as hell," she admitted, leaning back in her seat. "Not my idea, but eh, worth a shot, right?"

Alex's eyes widened, suddenly realizing what she was saying. "My brake lines? Really?"

She shrugged. "Not my idea. I don't do shitty ideas."

"And let me guess, you guys stole my phone too."

"Look at me, Rico. Tie my hair back, put on a little makeup, I could be a rich little college student too, you know. No one was going to pay attention. I could watch you all I wanted. So yeah, took the phone. Nice password, by the way."

"The one you didn't manage to crack," Alex said, guessing wildly.

She huffed. "Which is why I said it was nice. The

picture on the lock screen was cute, though. I'll give you that much."

"Shut your fucking mouth," Alex snarled at her, taking a step forward.

The men behind him only twitched, but Sofia was far faster. In a flash, there was a gun in her hand, leveled at Alex's chest. He knew enough about her to know there was probably a knife or two hidden somewhere in her clothes as well. Sofia De La Cruz wasn't just an administrator for the family. She occasionally moonlighted as one of the more vicious and capable enforcers as well.

Alex continued to glare at her. "Don't talk about my brother. None of you get to talk about my brother, you understand me? You want me, you got me. Try to have your sick little fucking games with me all you want, but leave everyone else out of this."

"Including the pretty boy?" she asked, sounding far too pleased with herself.

"Yes," Alex ground out.

Sofia leaned back in her seat, propping up her feet to get comfortable. "I've gotta be honest with you, Rico, I was a little surprised when we found out you were a fag. Especially from some of the stories my girls liked to tell me."

"Congrats," he sneered at her. "You learned that people can wanna fuck both. Have fun with that."

"Gotta say, though, your taste in boy toys is just as surprising. I mean, he's just so wholesome. How the hell did you land that?"

"With my charming personality."

She snorted. "Right, because you're just overflowing with charm, aren't you? Then again, from the stories my girls liked to tell me, I'm guessing you won him over with a certain somethin' else."

Alex glared at her as Sofia's eyes drifted down to his crotch. "The fuck do you care anyway? Fag or not, you're not here to fuck me."

"Well, not anymore. Though, given the chance back in the day," Sofia hummed thoughtfully, grinning wide. "Definitely. But you're right, that's not why we're here, and even if you weren't a backstabbing traitor, I wouldn't let you put that dick in me now. Your man might be pretty, but I don't let nothing but real men fuck me."

Now he understood and he could only shake his head. "It's not going to work, Sofia."

She raised a brow. "What's that?"

"You're not going to get a rise out of me. Insult me all you want, insult him for being into guys all you want, call us every name under the sun, and constantly remind me that you know about him," he shrugged. "I'm here, I'm already fucked, and we both know it. So why don't you cut to the very end of this bullshit? I've done my part of the deal. I'm here and on time. Now you do yours, let Cid go."

"Well, I do consider myself a woman of my word," she said slowly, though that twisted smile hadn't left her face.

Alex closed his eyes, knowing it had been too much to hope that she would have followed through on the deal. In reality, that had been why he'd messaged Ken in the first place. Alex had no doubt he probably wasn't going to get out of this building alive, but if he could make sure the cavalry arrived in time to save Cid, then he'd succeeded.

One of the men pushed past him, bending over to murmur in her ear. Her eyes narrowed, and the man tapped the side of his head, where Alex could see an earpiece nestled in his ear.

"What?" she growled, pushing herself up. "You two, stay here. He tries anything, shoot him in the dick for all I care but don't kill him. Antonio wants him personally. Have the other two meet me at the bottom of the stairs."

"Wha..." Alex began but was pushed aside roughly by Sofia and left to stand in the office by himself.

He had no idea what was happening, but the change in Sofia had been immediate. Alex knew enough about her reputation to know her temper was even more dangerous than her brother's, and few people wanted to risk her ire.

Alex knew that whoever had pissed her off better hope she didn't get her hands on them.

CID

Cid did not know a whole lot about what was happening. He didn't know precisely where he was or who the people who'd kidnapped him were. That ignorance did nothing for the gnawing panic that threatened to claw its way out of his chest. Which is why after what he thought was an hour, he had started focusing on what he did know.

He knew he was being kept in some small, dirty room, probably out of the way of anyone who might hear him. Cid thought it might have once been a storeroom of some sort if the fragments of boxes and shelves around the edges of the room were any indication.

Also, he knew that while they weren't terribly afraid of him, they were still cautious enough to leave someone in the room with him. A tall, if somewhat emaciated, man with dark eyes held a bright, frantic light Cid wasn't too comfortable with. The man, Luis, was Cid's only point of contact with the group, and it was from him that he'd managed to puzzle out more of the mystery.

They were looking for Alex, who they kept referring to

as Rico, so Cid had to assume it was a case of mistaken identity or Rico was Alex's real name. Since he didn't know for sure, Cid decided to keep internally referring to him by the name he'd always known. Whatever his name was, they wanted Alex badly, and they weren't looking to give him a nice present when they got a hold of him either.

Across the room, Luis fidgeted in the rickety chair he'd dragged into the room. It looked a lot more comfortable than the floor Cid had been left on, even more so when he considered the ropes tied around his ankles and wrists.

"You're looking a little pale," Cid told him, realizing the man had lost color since the last time he'd paid attention to him.

"Fuck you," Luis muttered, fingers nervously tapping at the pocket of his cargo pants.

It was the sort of reaction he would have expected from the other man. Most of Luis's conversation involved a great deal of swearing, though he'd been less tense when Cid had first talked to him.

"Shit don't last," Luis muttered to himself. "Ain't no good. Can't believe they gave me shit."

Cid decided he might as well risk it. "What?"

Luis shot him a poisonous glare. "Shut your mouth, tired of hearing you."

Cid shrugged and did as he was told. As much as he was willing to risk the man swearing at him, he really didn't want to get hit again. They hadn't been shy about it, and his face and torso ached. And while he knew it was a bad idea to self-diagnose, he didn't think he had any internal injuries or a concussion.

Luis fidgeted again, finally reaching into his cargo pants and drawing out a box and a small bottle. The bottle was set on a ragged-looking shelf beside Luis, and though Cid couldn't read the label, he would bet money that it didn't contain insulin. Just like he was sure the needles from the box weren't for medicinal purposes.

The other man fumbled with a needle, his fingers jittering and shaking as he tried to get it into the bottle. Cid watched the syringe fill with the fluid from the bottle, Luis stopping at a certain point and setting the bottle aside. And to his horror and amusement, Cid watched as the man searched his arm for somewhere to stick it.

"Well," Cid hear himself say. "That's your problem."

"Don't fucking judge me, fag," Luis hissed.

Cid ignored the jab. He'd already heard it enough times in the past few hours that he was immune. "I don't mean that you're doing drugs. But you're not gonna get much out of it injecting it that way."

"And how would you fucking know?"

"I'm a doctor. I'm not exactly a stranger to needles or injecting people."

Luis narrowed his eyes at him. "And where should I be putting it then, Mr. Doctor?"

Cid had only been rambling when he'd been correcting Luis, but he realized with a flash of inspiration that he might have given himself the chance he needed.

He leaned forward, squinting. "Hard to tell from here, but it's looking like you're kind of out of luck when it comes to your arms. If you want that stuff to hit you fast, which, based on your tremors and pale complexion, I'm guessing you do, you want an artery."

"And where the fuck is that?"

"Best ones are the neck and groin."

Luis's eyes widened. "I ain't takin' off my pants you..."

Cid shook his head. "Neck works just as good."

"I can't see my neck!"

Cid rolled his eyes. "I can guide you."

Luis snorted. "Don't pull nothin'."

"A needle wouldn't be able to kill you anyway, even if you did jab yourself badly," Cid assured him.

It turned out Luis had waited a little too long for his next hit. The man's hands were shaking so badly, even as Cid tried to patiently help the man maneuver the needle around to find the right spot. And while Cid was growing slightly impatient, Luis was steadily losing his temper as the needle's point jumped, weaved, and ended up nowhere near where Cid was trying to lead him.

Luis swore, half in English, and half in Spanish, when he managed to jab himself in the Adam's Apple, and with a jerk of his hand, sent the needle onto the ground, breaking the casing around it.

"No offense," Cid told him slowly. "But your hands are shaking too much to do something like this, and it would be hard enough to jab yourself in the neck right with steady hands."

"Then you fucking do it!" Luis snarled at him, holding a hand to his throat.

"You want...me, to inject you with...I don't even know what it is."

Luis hissed. "Do it or so help me fucking God, I don't care what Sofia says, I'll beat you down."

Cid held up his bound hands in placation. "Alright, alright. I'll do it, I guess."

Which was even better than his original plan of hoping the rush of drugs would make Luis a little more pliant and off-guard. He pushed himself to his feet, wobbling as he shuffled his way to Luis and grabbed the bottle and a needle from the box.

"Turn to the side and tilt your head," Cid told him as he read the bottle.

Ketamine? Jesus, he didn't even know people still did that recreationally. Yet, he knew enough to have a good idea about dosages, at least as much as he possibly could. Luis was not a horse, resistance was a factor, and he couldn't be totally sure about the man's weight either. And wouldn't be able to ask without being suspicious.

Still, he had seen enough to know about what line the man had filled it to before and using that as a gauge, stuck the needle into the bottle and pulled on the plunger. Luis watched him out of the corner of his eyes, but he seemed more intent on watching Cid's general movements rather than precisely what he was doing. Considering the man hadn't said a word when the syringe was filled with more than the man had used before, Cid guessed he either didn't know or just didn't care.

Feeling a little sick at what he was doing, he found the spot and jabbed the needle in. It would have been so easy to put air into the needle, but damn, he didn't want to kill the man. He was still running the risk, but as he stepped back, getting out of range of the other man, Cid thought it was better than outright murder.

Hating himself still, he tossed the needle to the side, away from both of them. In the few minutes it took for him to take his seat on the floor again, he could see the effect of the drug on Luis's system. The man gave a shudder, eyelids fluttering closed as he sighed deeply.

"Fuck, you weren't kidding," Luis said thickly. "I was doin' it wrong."

"It looked like a normal dosage on the bottle," Cid told him, keeping the conversation up to monitor Luis's reactions.

"Fuck yeah," Luis said, sounding pleased.

That pleasure lasted for only a few minutes more, and Cid watched as the man tried to sit up. Rather than going upright, however, the man nearly flopped onto his face, barely catching himself in time.

"The fuck?" Luis said, voice so thick and heavy it was barely understandable. "No, no, too strong. Fuck."

"Too much?" Cid heard himself ask as Luis's muscles gave up the fight and spilled him face-first onto the ground.

"Fucker," Luis grunted, trying to reach out toward Cid but succeeding only in wiggling his arm. "You motherfucker."

Cid was quite sure the man had no right to despise him. They'd kidnapped him, beaten him, and probably wouldn't think twice about killing him if that wasn't their plan from the start. Put into that sort of situation, anyone with half a living survival instinct would have gladly done the same.

Luis continued to mutter, though he quickly became unintelligible. When Cid was sure the man couldn't move, let alone pose a threat to him, he finally got up. Luis barely twitched, though he grumbled something when Cid searched his belt, grunting when he found the knife in its sheath on the front of the man's pants.

It went a long way toward getting the ropes off a lot easier for Cid. It took some wriggling of his hands to cut the ones around his wrists without slicing his skin open, but the ones around his ankles went quickly.

"Doing alright down there?" Cid asked, toeing the man with his shoe and getting no response.

Sighing, he crouched beside Luis, pressing his fingers to the man's neck. His pulse was sluggish, but Cid thought it seemed pretty even. It didn't look like Luis was in immediate danger, but Cid didn't have the time or the desire to stand around and make sure. He had seen Luis talking into an earpiece earlier, so he knew it was only a matter of time before someone noticed the man's silence.

The only door to the room led out into a dark hallway, one apparently littered with debris as Cid tried to quietly make his way through it. He found a set of stairs and carefully made his way up them, not wanting to make a lot of noise and trying to avoid accidentally breaking something.

He emerged into a huge room filled with rusted, broken-down machinery. Looking up, he realized he was in a factory of some sort. Cid couldn't remember if there was even a factory near Greenford, so he still had no idea where he was.

The sound of a harsh voice sent him scuttling behind one of the machines. A woman, whose voice he recognized, and two men marched down the aisle between the machinery.

"I swear," she ground out. "If that worthless pendejo is out of his head, I'm putting a bullet in it."

"He's pretty smart about not doing it on the job, not too heavily," one of the men added.

A thump of metal and Cid could see them descending through a gap in the machine he was using as cover. "Chingado! Shouldn't be doing it at all while he's working."

Cid knew he didn't have much time left, as the room he'd been in hadn't been far from the steps. The problem was, he didn't know which direction to go. For all he knew, the building had a lot more people in it who would have been more than willing to drag him back to his cell or even put a bullet in his brain to save themselves the trouble.

The room he was in wasn't very well lit. There were only a few dim bulbs and the light of the moon coming through the broken windows higher up in the room. Cid knew the direction the woman and her buddies had come from, but he wasn't so sure if that was the direction he wanted to go. Then again, going deeper into the building in an even more unfamiliar direction didn't exactly sound like the best idea either because he knew even less about what he might walk into.

A loud, shrieking voice boiled up from the tunnel he had just exited. "I want that little maricon found now!"

Indecision wasn't going to get him out alive and Cid dashed in the direction the three had originally come from. Using the little amount of light coming into the room, he did his best to dodge stray pieces of machinery, jumping over them when he could see them littered on the ground. As he darted down the aisle, he could see a dim light somewhere up ahead and on the next floor. The stairs leading up to the light were only a few feet away, and Cid hoped that was where he needed to go, or he was in trouble.

And with a sudden crash and a boom, the entire place descended into chaos.

Glass rained down from up above and he heard more shouting and banging. Cid scrambled for the stairs, desperate to get up them as gunshots rang out.

"Holy shit," Cid barked as a few bullets hit the stairs and then the doorway he was barreling toward.

"Hold them off!" he heard the woman shriek, her voice echoing through the factory.

"Down! Get down on the ground!" a different, far more

masculine voice boomed out, and it was chorused by several others.

Cid had no idea what was happening, but he knew the chaos was coming toward him. He scrambled up the stairs, only to be met by two men heading toward him. Cid gulped as one of them raised his gun, his scarred lip curling into an ugly smile.

And then the man grunted as a hunk of metal came from behind and slammed into the side of his head, sending him reeling. Cid slid to a stop, gaping as Alex spun, slamming the metal bar into the other man's side, and Cid winced when he heard the crack of the man's ribs. Alex didn't waste any time, taking advantage of the second man's pain to bring the rod down on his back, sending him sprawling.

"Stay down," Alex grunted, giving the man a swift kick to the head, making it bounce off the ground, stilling him.

"Fucking hell," Cid said, holding his hand up to his chest as his heart raced.

Alex's eyes blazed as they looked at him. "Christ, Cid, are you okay?"

"Other than watching you beat the shit out of two guys like it was nothing?" Cid asked faintly. "Yeah, I'm great. I'm fine. Also, what the hell is going on?"

More yelling and gunshots echoed from below, growing closer, making Alex wince. "Uh, that would be the cavalry that I called. Though I did tell Ken to go quiet, asshole."

"Your babysitter?" Cid asked in disbelief.

"Uh, witness protection?"

"Is that a question?"

"Is this really the time?"

"Yes! Yes it is, Alex...Rico, whatever the hell your name is!"

Alex stepped closer, reaching out slowly to Cid. "Look, I promise you, after this, I'll tell you everything. But we have to get out of sight before they end up spilling up here and..."

His rushed words were cut off as another bang, far too close for Cid's comfort, brought their attention around. One of the men from before, along with the woman, her hair flying crazily in every direction, stumbled to the top of the stairs. She was clutching a handgun in one hand and yanking the other man with her.

"Fuck," Alex hissed, trying to grab Cid to drag him back.

She spun around, spying them. "You!"

Cid felt his whole body go rigid as the woman raised the gun, spinning it around to aim at them. He had no idea who it was meant for, but he found himself unable to do anything but stare helplessly at the pit of black that made up the barrel of the gun.

Alex, however, was a lot quicker.

Yelping in surprise, Cid felt himself grabbed roughly and yanked back off his feet as the retort of the gun filled the office space. His back hit the ground just as Alex landed on top of him, managing to catch himself with his hands. From behind them, Cid could see more men, these ones armored and wielding far more dangerous weapons, barreling up the stairs, tackling the screaming woman and the other man to the ground.

Alex winced. "You okay?"

"I don't think she got me," Cid said, reaching up to touch Alex and going rigid when he felt warmth spread over his palm. "Alex?"

"I don't think I was so lucky," Alex grunted, limply slumping to the side.

"Alex!" Cid cried out, following him over.

Immediately, he could see the wound in the man's side, already thick with blood. Alex gave a harsh grunt as he reached out to touch him and then, remembering what was happening, hesitated. After a moment's thought, Cid ripped off his outer shirt and then the T-shirt underneath. It wouldn't be the cleanest thing, but it was far more hygienic than anything else he had to hand.

"Alex," Cid told him, pressing the balled-up shirt against the man's wound tightly. "Going to need you to breathe for me, alright? I need your heart rate to go down a little bit."

"Oh yeah, I'll just calm down real quick, perfect place for it," Alex said between gritted teeth.

"Think of it as urban exploring," Cid told him, hating the sight of Alex's blood coating his hand. "We're having a nice little illegal bit of exploring. And you're perfectly calm."

"You can't paint a picture for shit," Alex told him.

"Sir," one of the armored men said, approaching with his gun raised. "Put your hands in the air and step away."

Cid glanced at him and then the gun. He raised a brow and looked down. "Do you see what I'm doing? I'll remove my hands when you get a goddamn medic in here, and there had better be an ambulance on the way with all this firepower."

"Sir," the man began.

"No," Cid told him calmly. "It's not happening."

Alex chuckled, wincing as he did it. "I don't know which of Ken's cronies you are, but it's fine. He's probably the only one here who hasn't hurt a fly in his life."

As if on cue, he heard a shot from below. "We got one in the lower level. Out cold."

Cid winced. "Maybe not completely true anymore."

Alex stared up at him, eyes glassy. "What...did you do?"

Cid's attention snapped back to him. "Alex, hey, don't do that. I need you to stay awake."

"I'm here," Alex said, voice betraying his weakness.

"Alex!" Cid called down as the man's eyelids fluttered. "Someone, get a medic up here, help me!"

ALEX/RICO

"Gotta say, getting stabbed hurt a hell of a lot more," Rico snorted, wincing when the movement jarred his wounded side. "But recovering from getting shot is the worst."

Standing at the end of the hospital bed, Ken glared at him. "You not getting shot or stabbed was the entire point of bringing you into the program."

"Yeah, and look how well that turned out," Rico grumbled. Wincing once more as he jabbed a finger at Ken. "I thought you said everything was quiet."

"It was. We were wrong," Ken said, which was probably the closest Rico was going to get to an apology.

"Please tell that to my spleen," Rico grumbled.

Beside the bed, Cid stirred restlessly. "It was your kidney."

"Is there a difference?"

"Medically speaking, yes. For what you're aiming for? Probably not."

Honestly, Rico was a little surprised Cid was even in the room with him and downright shocked that Ken had allowed it. Then again, when Rico had woken up that first day, it had been to the sight of Cid glaring at a red-faced Ken. Neither of them had told Rico what had happened, but somehow, he thought some of the spirit he'd witnessed from Cid in the factory had come out once again.

"It looks as though you'll be discharged sometime in the next couple of days," Ken told him, his eyes darting toward Cid. "After that, we'll have to discuss what we're going to do with you next."

"What about Sofia?" Rico asked. He'd been left to stew in the bed for two days without any information and he thought it was about time.

"In custody, and we're not letting her go for anything. Unless we get an inept or corrupt judge, we can bet on her not getting bail. Most of the crew she had with her is dead, though a couple of them survived," Ken explained.

Cid let out a deep sigh. "What about Luis?"

"Luis Everett?" Ken asked neutrally. "One of the survivors, though by a technicality."

Cid winced at that. "Do I want to know?"

Ken eyed him. "Do you?"

"Just tell me," Cid groaned. "You really do play too many mind games."

Again, Rico was left to wonder what exactly had happened while he was unconscious. He knew the medics had got to him, and once they'd loaded him in the ambulance, with Cid right behind in the truck, they'd managed to get him to the hospital. Cid had told him everything, looking paler and more drawn than Rico had ever seen him, including that it had been a close thing and that while surgery had saved his life, it could have easily gone badly.

"He's stable. They're not sure when he'll wake up, if at all. Apparently, overdoses can be a little tricky for some people, particularly long-time users," Ken told him matter of factly.

Cid put his head down on the bed, taking a deep breath. Rico reached out, taking hold of the man's hand and squeezing it.

"Ass," Rico accused Ken.

Ken looked unimpressed by the assessment. "If he wanted to know, I saw no point in sugar-coating it. I know this sort of thing can be difficult for someone who isn't used to violence or having to take extreme measures to preserve their own life. But Cedric was under clear and foreign duress and still managed to operate with a clear head and quick thinking. And from his own story, he even tried to make sure not to kill the man, which would have been easy to do."

"Wait," Rico looked up, frowning. "Your name is Cedric?"

Cid looked down, the guilt on his face disappearing under a burst of laughter. "Yes you dork! What did you think Cid was short for?"

"I didn't know it was short for anything," Rico told him, annoyance in his voice. "You never told me that."

Cid shook his head. "And you never told me your name was really Rico."

"That's not fair," Rico told him.

"Maybe. But it's also the truth."

Rico scowled at him, even as he was privately relieved to see the smile back on Cid's face. Back at the factory, he'd thought the last thing he was going to see was the panicked and terrified expression on Cid's face. While he didn't think it would have been such a bad thing, seeing Cid's face before going, he would have preferred the happy and bright expression that looked so at home on it instead.

Ken cleared his throat. "That being said, I'm sure the two of you have a great deal to discuss."

"Oh, what, am I going to be left alone for more than a minute?" Rico asked crossly.

"Your boyfriend was kidnapped, attacked, and you were coerced into giving yourself up to people who would have happily tortured you both before killing you," Ken reminded him. "Forgive me if I wanted to make sure there was always someone around you while you recovered."

Rico winced at that, but mostly at the reminder of what had almost happened to him and Cid. Ken had once tried to warn him that his association with Cid might put him in danger, but Rico hadn't wanted to listen.

"Sorry," Rico muttered, squeezing Cid's fingers apologetically. "You're right."

"We'll keep a couple of men posted outside the door," Ken told him. "You'll have your privacy to talk."

"Thank you, Agent Drayfus," Cid called after him.

Ken waved a hand over his shoulder. "Might as well start calling me Ken as well. Good night gentlemen."

Rico turned his head sharply toward Cid. "What was that about?"

Cid shrugged. "He and I uh...didn't agree on the arrangements he was trying to carry out."

"Yeah, I've been trying to get you both to tell me what the hell I woke up to a couple of days ago," Rico reminded him.

Cid sniffed indignantly. "You'd just woken up after being shot, almost dying, and going through surgery, all within the past twenty-four hours. I was a little more concerned about your immediate recovery than I was to tell you everything that happened. It just so happens that Agent Drayfus apparently agreed with me on that point."

"Okay, fine, Doc, I'm apparently not going to bleed out on you now," Rico said. "So how about you tell me what that was about?"

"First of all," Cid said, narrowing his eyes. "Don't make jokes about that. It's not funny."

"Fine," Rico admitted, nodding his head. "Not funny for you. Got it."

Cid huffed. "He wanted to move me to a separate location after I'd been examined. I refused both requests."

"Wait, you didn't get looked at? Are you serious?"

"I'm a doctor, Alex...Rico. I think I can assess my own injuries well enough. I was far more concerned with your status than with a few bumps and bruises."

Rico scowled at him. "You better be fuckin' joking, because if you didn't let someone look at you..."

Unbelievably, Cid jutted his lip forward. "Yes. I did."

"Why are you...are you pouting?"

"Maybe."

"Why?"

Cid muttered something that Rico couldn't understand.

"What?" he asked, trying to lean closer.

"I got bullied by the nurses," Cid finally said, huffing. "They wouldn't let me into your room because of how dirty I was, said it was an infection risk. Then when I tried to get changed, they pulled me into the room and refused to let me leave until they'd done an exam. It was brutal."

Rico tried not to laugh, and not just because it hurt his side to do so. It was really the pain that kept his laughter at bay, however, because Cid looked completely pitiful.

"I shouldn't think it," Rico said, reaching out to brush a finger over Cid's bruised cheek. "But you are kinda cute when you're pouting."

Cid huffed. "Anyway. I didn't want to be put somewhere else, even if it was for 'safekeeping.' I'm not a piece of expensive china. And secondly, why would I go somewhere else when there's already going to be guys with guns watching you, so I'd be safe here. Ken didn't agree, I didn't agree with him, we argued."

"I'm kinda mad I didn't get to see that," Rico admitted. "Even I've never argued that hard with him before."

Cid shrugged. "We came to a little bit of an agreement after that."

Rico's finger rested on Cid's cheek, the dark marks sending another stab of guilt into his gut. "Are you okay? I mean it."

Cid chuckled, turning his cheek into Rico's hand. "You're the one who got shot, remember?"

"Cid. I mean it."

The man smiled at him. "I know. But I don't know what to tell you. I've never been in a situation like that before. Never had dangerous people threaten my life or...try to kill me or someone I care about. Also never drugged someone into a coma either...well, actually, not on purpose, that is. There's certainly a possibility that I could have done it in the past and never knew it...does making someone at a frat party get way too drunk with you and pass out for twelve hours count?"

"No, that sounds like a party," Rico said, starting to grin as Cid continued.

"And of course there's finding out that you weren't like, some deadly assassin hiding from your enemies, or that you were some prince on the run from an attempted coup trying to wipe out the last of your line, that was something too."

Rico squinted at him. "I...what?"

Cid waved him off. "Alice, some joke she made when I talked to her after Saturday."

"You talked to her about us?" Rico wondered.

"Yeah, she'd be...ridiculously mad, probably at both of us, but herself too if she knew. I went to your apartment to talk to you about the whole thing, maybe try to figure things out. But uh, surprise, those people were there instead and they grabbed me," Cid said, words coming out at Mach five.

Rico held up his hand. "They were at my apartment?"

"Yes."

"Where you were."

"Yes."

"Looking for me."

"Yes."

"To talk to me...about?"

Cid let out a breathy laugh. "What else? Us. What was going on, or what couldn't go on or whatever it was that we needed to talk about. After everything you said, I realized it just didn't sit right with me, leaving things as they were. I wanted you to know that even if you had this big secret you couldn't tell, I still wanted to be with you. Even with that secret, it didn't change who you were. You were still Alex."

"Well," Rico began, grimacing. "Not really."

Cid rolled his eyes, prodding Rico in the shoulder. "Fine, not Alex, you're Rico, whatever. My point was that I wanted to tell you that no matter what, you were still the man I had come to know, the one who made me open my big fat mouth and tell you I was falling for you."

Which left only one thing to really discuss between the two of them, and Rico braced himself for it.

"And now you know the truth I'd been keeping secret," Rico said softly.

Cid hummed thoughtfully. "Not...all of it."

"With what you do know...do you really want to know the rest?" Rico asked, taking a deep breath.

Cid peered up at him, nodding slowly. "Yeah, I think I do. All things considered."

Rico couldn't blame him for that. If he were in the man's shoes, he would have been anxious for answers as well. The only place was to start from the top, from when he'd taken his first job for the Los Muertos to get the bills paid and electric turned back on, and how that had started a new career for him.

"It wasn't about the money," Rico told him, squeezing Cid's fingers in a desperate bid for him to understand. "But where we were, if you didn't have the protection, you were pretty much free game for everyone. I wanted us safe, my brother and me."

He had done his best to stick to jobs that wouldn't keep him up at night. That didn't always work, though, and Rico had seen things, things he wouldn't try to describe to Cid. Sometimes he'd had to hurt people, ones who posed a threat, both to him and others, and there had been more than a few fights and threats.

And there had been more than threats.

Rico had wanted his brother to be as clean of that life as he possibly could and made his brother swear up and down that he would. Rico hadn't known that his little brother had got the same idea in his head and tried to do his part as well. It was the only reason Rio would have *ever* done something like that, that he knew.

"And it...that choice," Rico's voice faltered then, his throat threatening to close on him as he tried to get the story out.

Gunned down on the street. Bleeding out in the gutter like he was a stray. His brother was supposed to be protected, but the Los Muertos had let him into their circle and sent him to the wolves.

"And that's when you went witness?" Cid asked, voice tight.

"They killed him," Rico told him in a choked voice. "They didn't pull the fucking trigger themselves, but they fucking killed him. He was my little brother, Cid, my little goddamn brother. I held that little shit when he was a baby, I held him when he cried during the night, I made sure he ate, went to school. I was the one who took him to the doctor's when he got pneumonia when our crackhead mom couldn't be bothered to get off the couch. He was my brother, he was my *everything*, and they fucking killed him."

Grief, sharp, glassy, and infinite in its hunger, consumed him. He couldn't remember the last time he'd cried, maybe when he was a kid. There had been no tears when he'd heard about Rio or when he'd gone to his brother's funeral. There had been no tears when he'd left home or when he'd been forced to start all over.

It felt as if all those tears had built up inside him, waiting until the pressure was too intense. He barely noticed the pain in his side as he curled up, trying to wrap himself around Cid as the man held him, sobs wracking Rico's body as he mourned for the man who had been both brother and son to him.

It ripped through him like a storm, tearing up all the willpower and strength he had left inside. And eventually, it left him feeling hollow and exhausted, curled up on his side, unable to summon the will to lift his arm or say another word.

"Sleep," Cid whispered to him gently, running a hand over his face. "I'll be here when you wake up. I'll stay with you."

Rico closed his hand over Cid's, holding it desperately

as he tried to cling to that promise as he let himself not so much drift as plunge into the abyss of dreamless sleep.

———

WHEN HE AWOKE SOMETIME LATER, bleary-eyed and groggy, he wasn't surprised to find he was alone in the room. Some part of him hadn't expected Cid to sit around and wait for him to wake up. Not after everything Rico had told him, and he honestly wouldn't be surprised if the man had decided to fly halfway across the country rather than have to be in the same room.

It didn't ease the ache in his chest any less.

"Ah, you're awake, good," Ken's familiar voice piped up from the doorway. "That means we can get to discussing future accommodations."

Rico rolled onto his back, eyeing the man. "Alright, where are you locking me up? And do I get to know where the key is?"

"Cute," Ken said dryly, pulling out his phone and peering over the screen. "Though not completely far from the truth. As it stands, we need to get you somewhere that we are completely certain does not have ties to the Los Muertos."

"And where the fuck is that?" Rico demanded. "Canada?"

"Close actually, we're thinking Northern Maine. There's a rather nice town up that way that will serve our purposes nicely. There will be a little bit more paperwork and shuffling around of things to accommodate, but we can certainly manage it," Ken paused to look Rico over. "And some winter gear as well. As nice as the summers can be there, the winters are absolutely brutal."

"Oh boy," Rico said dryly.

Ken raised a brow. "Problem?"

Rico looked down at the sheets, jaw tightening. "No."

He didn't have a right to complain and they both knew it. They had tried to do it his way, and he'd almost got himself and someone completely innocent killed in the process. At this point, he was surprised he was even being told what was going to happen.

"And being that the location is pretty out of the way, you won't have to worry about keeping your head down quite as much," Ken told him. "Though we will be keeping a small team nearby at a different house just in case."

"At least I won't be lonely," Rico said, shrugging.

Ken looked up, a puzzled expression on his face. "The entire point of the cohabitation was to alleviate social isolation, provide an emotional boost, and hopefully provide a little bit of counterbalance to your unique personal difficulties."

Rico scowled at him. "I have to live with the team? Damn it, I should've known."

Ken let his phone drop, cocking his head. "What..."

Cid stepped into the room, clutching a plastic bag and a monstrous cup of steaming coffee in the other hand. "We uh, didn't get a chance to talk about it yet. So, kind of still need to hear his input on it. Sorry, Agent Drayfus, he fell asleep before it could happen."

Rico's chest loosened at the sight of the man. Though the bruises were still an ugly reminder of what had happened, there seemed to be a buoyancy to him that had disappeared after the factory incident. The fact that the bag in his hand also happened to be filled with a large array of candy added to that impression.

Ken sighed, looking up toward the ceiling. "Thank God I came in here before I started getting the ball rolling."

"What is going on?" Rico asked, glancing between the two men.

"Considering we took Sofia De La Cruz into custody, as well as a few of her men, Cedric presents something of a problem," Ken began. "And something of a solution."

"She saw my face," Cid said, sitting on the edge of the bed at Rico's side. "Knows my name, everything there is to know for her to be able to find me. Or have someone else find me."

"And he is one of the only witnesses to her crimes," Ken continued.

Cid nodded, pulling out a bag of Skittles and pouring some into his hand. "Which makes me like, double on her hitlist. Skittles?"

Rico eyed the handful of colorful candy. "You're telling me I got you dragged into this shit completely?"

Cid shrugged. "Don't blame yourself."

Both Rico and Ken snorted at that, drawing another eye roll out of Cid.

"Anyway," Cid said loudly before anyone could continue. "They kind of are in a bind because...well, they need me to testify, just like they need you to. So when it comes right down to it..."

"Cedric is officially being brought into the program as well," Ken finished, eyeing Cid's candy.

Cid, catching his eye, held the bag out to the agent. "And because the two of us are pretty much needed to be witnesses for at least one of the same crimes, we can be lumped together. Well, and it also makes it like, a lot cheaper too."

Ken nodded, popping a few pieces into his mouth. "I

won't pretend money isn't a motivation. If we can manage to save from having to house, fund, and protect another person and have two under one roof, we most certainly will."

"But they have this whole thing where they want to make sure everyone living together is cool with it," Cid said, again holding the candy out to the agent, who again accepted some. "Which is why we're talking now."

"You want us...to live together?" Rico asked Ken.

"It would be simpler," Ken said, popping another Skittle into his mouth. "Cheaper, easier to watch, and if it keeps you both calm, happy, and willing to cooperate, all the better."

"And you?" Rico asked Cid.

Which earned a laugh as Cid's bright blue eyes lit up with his amusement. "I wouldn't have agreed to it if I wasn't ready to do it. Plus, they're going to set me up to be able to work through the little clinic they have in town. I'll be able to do my job, under a fake name...and credentials apparently."

"We can't use your real name on them," Ken pointed out. "But considering you have the education and training necessary, the only thing fake about them is the name and dates."

"Yeah, I guess," Cid muttered, not looking convinced.

"After all this shit," Rico said, ignoring their conversation and focusing on Cid. "You want to stay with me?"

"Ah," Ken said, tucking his phone away. "That's my cue."

"Hey!" Cid called, tossing a bag of candy at the man before he left the room. "Might as well take that with you."

Rico decided to ignore that his taciturn and overly serious babysitter had a sweet tooth. "Cid?"

The blond man turned to him, giving him a dazzling smile. "I mean, if you want it, yeah, definitely."

"After everything?" Rico repeated.

Cid laughed. "Everything? You were supposed to be safe and in the clear. Even Ken admitted that they never knew danger was so close. It was no one's fault what happened, except for the people that did it. I don't hold that against you, and I'm not going to."

"And what I told you?" Rico asked, his heart pounding.

Cid cocked his head, frowning in confusion. "What about it?"

"That...didn't bother you?"

"Oh. Well, yeah, I guess it did...does. It's kind of hard to picture you doing those sorts of things, but it's not hard to picture *why* you did them. If there was anything apparent last night, and for the past month, it's how much love you had for your brother."

A pang. Rico let it pass through him. "I guess."

Cid smiled sadly at him. "And it hurts that you had to do those things to make sure you both survived and that you had to go through all of that. And if I could trade what we have to get your brother back, I would do it in a heartbeat."

Rico swallowed hard, shaking his head. "It's not worth...thinking about."

"I know," Cid said, taking Rico's hand in his and holding on. "But after everything, what happened, what you told me, I realize I was right. You are exactly the sort of man I thought you were, whether your name is Alex, Rico, or whatever you end up with after you leave this hospital. You're still going to be a little too serious at times, overly sarcastic, a bit grumpy, but ultimately sweet and caring, a man who will do whatever it takes to take care of those who mean the most to them. A man who's endured a lot of pain and heartbreak but still finds it in himself to be a good person."

"Are we talking about you or me now?" Rico asked.

Cid laughed. "You. Because that's who you are."

Not for the first time, and he was sure it wouldn't be the last, Rico marveled at Cid's ability to bounce back and recover. He was sure there would be plenty of moments where things weren't quite as smooth or quite as easy. But there Cid was, despite everything he'd already been forced to endure because of Rico, still ready and willing to be with him.

"It gets really snowy in Maine, I hear," Rico said. "You sure you want to be locked up in a house with me for months on end?"

Cid leaned in, wrinkling his nose. "I think I should be the one asking *you* that. Do you know what I'm like when I'm cooped up and end up getting into way too much sugar?"

Rico looked down at the bag of candy. "I'm pretty sure I'm going to find out."

Cid hummed. "Well, maybe we should tell Agent Drayfus to wait a few hours before making a decision. Can't have you go Overlook Hotel on me in the middle of January."

"Go...what?" Rico asked in bewilderment.

Cid sighed heavily. "Another classic movie to add to the watch list. We might get through the whole thing by this time next year."

Rico reached up, gently cupping the man's face and turning it toward him. "You really want to do this?"

"I absolutely do," Cid told him, closing his fingers around Rico's wrist and squeezing.

Rico pulled him close then, pressing their lips together.

He didn't realize how long it had been since he'd last kissed the other man, but the familiar sensation washed through him as they stayed close.

If being with Cid meant more of this feeling, more of the constant feeling of relaxation, belonging, with a hefty dose of joy thrown in, how could Rico say no?

"Let's do it," Rico told him softly, grinning.

EPILOGUE

One Year Later

Andrew Merch, formerly Cedric Montray, pushed through the front door of his shared, two-story house. Despite being laden heavily with groceries in each hand, he carefully pulled off his shoes at the doorway and left them there. The Maine spring had turned out to be a wet one, and it felt like everything was completely covered in mud outside. Rico, who had once been Alex, and was now Curtis, was incredibly fussy about tracking mud in the house, and Cid didn't want to see the pained expression on the man's face if he saw him wearing muddy shoes indoors.

He paused before entering the kitchen, leaning into the living room from the nearby hallway.

"That you?" Rico called from somewhere upstairs.

"Nope, complete stranger," Cid called back, entering the kitchen to drop the groceries down. "I'm here to rob you."

It was nice to joke about. The first few months they'd been there, both of them had been a little tense and wary of strangers. Just under a year later, and there was a bit of ease to their lives now. Ken had told them it could take months, maybe even years, before big cases like theirs would end up at trial. And even when it was all said and done, they might have to stay in the program, as revenge was always a possibility. It seemed their lives were pretty much tied to the program for many years, and they had grown more comfortable with it over time.

"Well, I'm naked and wet, so I hope you like the show, random stranger," Rico called back in amusement.

Cid paused in his motion to grab the items out of the bag and start putting them away. He cocked his head, did a mental evaluation on how long it would be okay to leave them sitting out and made for the hallway. He reached the bottom of the stairs just in time for Rico to appear at the top.

"You are so wearing clothes!" Cid accused. "And you're not even wet. What the hell, man."

Rico chuckled, descending the stairs. "I can be naked and wet if you want me to be. It's not hard."

"But I like it hard," Cid said, smirking at him.

Rico wrapped an arm around Cid's waist and pulled him in for a hard kiss. "You're such a perv."

"You love it," Cid told him, chuckling when Rico squeezed his ass.

"I do," he said, letting Cid go and entering the kitchen. "I didn't expect you back for another couple of hours."

Cid chuckled, shaking his head. "Turns out Mrs. Panam's whole host of latest maladies was a dire case of...seasonal allergies. So I think she'll make it."

Rico chuckled, emptying the bags and stacking things on the counter. "Well, I still have to go down to Rich and

Lisa's house in a bit. Their furnace has been making that weird noise again and they want me to take a look at it for them."

One of the interesting quirks of fate had been to find out that Rico was incredibly handy around the house. Enough, apparently, to count as a resident handyman. Which had worked out well for him when they had been dropped off in Maine. Rico without anything to occupy his time.

It had been their neighbors who had made that discovery when Rico had offered to fix their porch light after mentioning it in passing. After that, any reluctance they'd had toward the strangers living at one end of town started to dwindle. That the other stranger happened to be a friendly, helpful, and apparently competent doctor, well that helped their reputation considerably.

And that they were two men, quietly living together? Not one word was said.

"Well," Cid said, grabbing the gallon of milk and the sticks of butter to put in the fridge. "Does that mean when you come back, you can get naked and wet? Preferably with me."

"I think I can manage that," Rico said, smirking at him as he handed over the orange juice.

It was amazing in its own way, how easily they had fit into one another's lives. That wasn't to say there weren't bad days because there were. Sometimes Cid woke up, covered in sweat and wondering if he was still in that room with a half-crazed drug addict. But Rico was always there, ready to hold him or to press a cold cloth over his head when he woke up panicked enough to puke.

And sometimes Rico would fall into a dark mood, obsessing over the past a little too much and angry at the world. On those days, Cid would let him be, let him walk the woods, and be there when Rico inevitably crawled into their bed, sometimes without a word, and pressed his face against Cid's chest, craving comfort.

So yeah, there were rough days, but they pushed through. Cid still managed to make Rico laugh and Rico sometimes got this little twinkle in his eyes when he thought Cid wasn't paying attention. And Rico still made Cid warm throughout his body, his voice still brought a smile to his face, and on the few occasions he laughed, Cid found it infectious.

"And you should probably take that time to write Alice," Rico pointed out, putting cans away. "Or she might end up storming the local government building."

"Oh. Shit. You're right," Cid grimaced. "It has been a little while."

Almost two weeks, in fact. Cid had been a little surprised to find there was a small grace period between agreeing to join the program and officially being put in it. He had been allowed to return to Greenford and tidy up his affairs. Ken had dealt with the university and whatever paperwork had been involved, and somewhere along the line, Dr. Finn had been told.

Dr. Finn had been waiting for him when he'd gone into the clinic after Rico had been released from the hospital. She hadn't been told much but apparently knew the government was involved and that had been enough for her. He knew it had killed her not to know what was going to happen to him, but the last couple of weeks he spent in Greenford, he'd made sure to see her, as well as promise her that he would be okay.

Telling Alice, however, had fallen on Cid. He was careful to leave out most of the details, but he had told her it was Witness Protection that was taking him and not Rico. Alice hadn't seen much of a difference, and along with some colorful insults toward Rico for the whole mess, she had hugged him fiercely and refused not to at least have email contact with him.

Apparently, that was perfectly fine. So long as Cid used a program installed on the house's computer, it could be sent anonymously to Alice and Dr. Finn, and anything they sent back would be routed through secure servers. And so, he'd kept in contact, mostly gossiping, but also just conversing and eventually, Alice had grown to forgive Rico for the entire affair.

Cid still didn't think she was a fan, though.

Rico stood up on the tips of his toes, reaching the top shelf to shove boxes of pasta up there. His shirt rode up, revealing his taut stomach and the fine hairs that made up his treasure trail. Cid grinned to himself as he watched, cocking his head.

Alice might not be a fan, but Cid was.

"Oh, I wonder if my download is done," Cid said aloud.

Rico looked askance at him. "Really? Write your email, or your ass is grass."

"Aw, babe, it's the new Hitman game," Cid whined. "I wanna play it."

"God, why is that cute?" Rico asked, sounding annoyed with himself. "I hate that I find that cute."

Cid slid next to him when he turned around, grinning up at him. "No you don't."

"I kinda do."

"Yeah, but like, in a good way."

The corner of Rico's mouth twitched. "Yeah, okay, in a good way."

Just like with their lives, Cid loved the way their bodies

just fit together. Cid had put on a few pounds of muscle from having to trek all over the place through thick snow, but Rico was as big as ever. Yet, no matter what, he always felt good, whether he was wrapped around Cid or the other way around.

"I'll even be good and have dinner ready by the time you get back," Cid promised him. "Try out my newfound cooking skills."

"Meaning you're going to pop a frozen lasagna into the oven," Rico smirked.

Damn it, that's exactly what he was going to do.

"It'll probably be a couple of hours, you know how Rick is when I come around," Rico said, kissing Cid. "He'll want to have a couple of beers and shoot the shit before I'm allowed to go."

Cid chuckled. "That's fine, but dinner will be cooked by eight, so be home by then if you want fresh food."

"Which is my perfect excuse to leave."

"And gives me plenty of time here too."

"To write Alice an email."

"Right. The email."

Rico rolled his eyes. "You're going to get us shot, and by your best friend at that."

Cid laughed, backing off so Rico could pull on and lace his boots for the half-mile walk down the road. "I'll write, I'll write. Also, for our movie tonight, something funny or something spooky?"

"Something with action wouldn't be bad," Rico told him as he stood up, boots on.

"Terminator it is then," Cid said, grinning. "Been waiting to show you this one."

"That's the one with the killer robots, isn't it?"

"Killer AI, and time-traveling, killer robots."

"Right."

Cid laughed, stretching upward to give Rico a kiss. "So it's a date."

"Dinner and movie at eight. I'll be there," Rico promised, opening the door. "You better be too. I hate being stood up."

"I'll be there," Cid told him. "Love you."

And just like the first time, and every time since he'd first said it to Cid, Rico stopped, looked up at Cid, and smiled as he said, "I love you too."

Cid watched him go down the street, arms crossed over his chest and a smile on his face. Theirs wasn't a life many people would wish for, and he was sure a lot of people would shy away from doing what they did. But as he watched Rico reach the end of the drive, turning to wave at Cid because he knew he'd be watching, Cid knew there was no other life for him.

Made in United States
North Haven, CT
12 October 2023